LIZARD'S TALE

Weng Wai Chan was born in Singapore and spent her childhood there. She now lives in Auckland with her husband and children. *Lizard's Tale* is her first book.

WENG WAI CHAN

TEXT PUBLISHING MELBOURNE AUSTRALIA

textpublishing.com.au
textpublishing.co.uk

The Text Publishing Company
Swann House, 22 William Street, Melbourne Victoria 3000, Australia

The Text Publishing Company (UK) Ltd
130 Wood Street, London EC2V 6DL, United Kingdom

Published by The Text Publishing Company, 2019
Reprinted 2020

Book design by Imogen Stubbs.
Cover and internal illustrations by Sarah Allen.
Typeset in Stempel Garamond by J&M Typesetting.

Printed and bound in Australia by Griffin Press, part of Ovato, an accredited ISO/NZS 14001:2004 Environmental Management System printer.

ISBN: 9781925603910 (paperback)
ISBN: 9781925626872 (ebook)

A catalogue record for this book is available from the National Library of Australia.

For my father, who grew up in Chinatown
And for my mother, who taught me to love books

CHAPTER ONE

Suite Seventy at Raffles Hotel

Tropical rain drummed on the red clay roof tiles of Raffles Hotel in Singapore. A skinny boy watched from below the balcony, hidden in the shrubbery, as a white-jacketed waiter hovered over the tables on the covered verandah. Silverware gleamed in the lamplight.

The boy beneath the balcony was called Lizard. The cool night rain soaked him right through, but he was used to that. At least it kept the mosquitoes away.

He watched his friend Roshan standing nervously beside the waiter. Roshan had just been promoted to dining room junior waiter, and he was terrified of making a mistake. Lizard winced as the waiter smacked Roshan's head.

'No, no, stupid boy!' said the waiter. 'The dessert spoon goes above the cake fork! Always, no exceptions. How many times must I tell you? Tonight's guests are very important—everything must be perfect!'

'Sorry, sir. I'll remember, sir,' stammered Roshan.

'*Tchah*! Go inside. I'll do this table myself.' The waiter gave Roshan a little push and Roshan scuttled off, past the large portrait of King George VI of England. It was 1940 and George VI had been king for three years.

Lizard hunched his shoulders, blinked the raindrops from his eyelashes and settled down to wait. He tucked his satchel close to keep it as dry as possible. He was thinking about how much he could make if he took just one of those gleaming forks to the Thieves' Market in Sungei Road, when finally he saw them come in and be shown to their table: Mr Sebastian Whitford Jones, general manager of the New British East India Company, and his wife, Jemima.

Lizard knew who they were, because he'd seen them arrive in their chauffeur-driven motor car earlier that afternoon. He had been waiting for them to come to dinner so that he could be sure they were not in their hotel suite.

'Jemima, darling, we're not too close to the rain here, are we?' asked Mr Whitford Jones, in a very loud, very English voice.

'Oh, no, Sebastian. This rain is so refreshing after the heat of today,' said Mrs Whitford Jones with a sigh.

Lizard was up and off, sprinting through the splatting raindrops. He sped through the wet blackness of the garden on bare feet, to suite seventy in the Palm Court wing. The Palm Court wing was double storey, but luckily suite seventy was on the ground floor. He ducked under one of the arches to the covered walkway. In a shadowy corner, he took his shirt off and squeezed it out, then used it to dry himself as best as he could. He shivered as he put the clammy shirt back on.

He peered through the half-opened window into an empty sitting room. Light filtered in from the overhead lamps of the passage way outside. His heart hammered as he opened the window further and slipped inside.

The wooden floorboards were smooth underfoot. He waited a moment, listening. A steady thrumming of ceiling fans came from the bedroom beyond. After a few more steps, his feet sank into plush Turkish carpet. He rubbed them on the soft pile, and ran his fingertips along the top of the plump brocade sofa as he moved past it.

He was looking for a bible-sized, plain teak box. Where could it be? Still in one of the leather- and brass-trimmed travelling trunks stacked up in the corner? He hoped not, because all three were padlocked. He tapped gently on their sides. They sounded hollow.

The antique Chinese sideboard? He pulled out a few drawers. Empty.

Maybe the writing desk? The drawers held only a fountain pen and some paper.

He glanced into the bedroom and saw two beds, each draped with mosquito netting that trembled in the breeze from the fans.

Lizard was about to creep in there to search when he remembered something. He looked back at the writing desk. Roshan had once shown him a secret drawer in a desk in a fancy suite just like this. Lizard crept to the desk, moved the heavy chair out of the way and crouched down. His nimble fingers explored the crevices under the desk, and he found it. He pressed the hidden catch and pulled out the drawer that appeared underneath. Here it was—a sturdy, oiled teak box. A thick metal ring held it shut.

That was easy. Maybe too easy.

Something nagged at him, telling him things weren't quite right. Best to get out quick, then, he thought. He shoved the box into his satchel and closed the secret drawer.

As he slipped out from under the desk and moved towards the open window, he realised what was wrong. The ceiling fans in the bedroom. Why would they be on if no one was in?

He didn't see the girl standing in the bedroom doorway watching him.

'Dinesh?' said the girl. 'Is that you, Dinesh?'

Lizard jumped. He whirled around just as she turned on the electric light. He blinked in the glare.

'Oh,' she said, looking at the skinny, soggy boy standing before her. 'I thought you were my friend, Dinesh. But you're not.' She stared at Lizard, as though blaming him for not being Dinesh. She had long, wavy, copper-coloured hair, large blue eyes and smooth pale skin. Lizard had never seen anyone so marvellously...clean.

'I'm terribly sorry,' Lizard gulped, though he wasn't quite sure what he was apologising for.

The girl's eyes widened, then narrowed. 'Well, you certainly don't sound like Dinesh, even though you dress like him,' she said, tilting her head. 'You sound more like...me.'

Lizard looked down at his old wet shirt, his too-large shorts and his dirty feet. His satchel hung in front of him and he clutched it tight as shame at his shabbiness bloomed hot in his chest.

'My friend Dinesh is Gujarati,' the girl said. 'He's the gardener's son back home in New Delhi. I'm not allowed to play with the servants' children, but they're the most fun. You're not Indian, though. What are you?'

'I'm…I don't know.' Lizard stared at the polished dark wood floor. He was leaving drops of water on it.

'You don't know?' The girl stifled a snort of laughter. 'Well, Master You-Don't-Know, how do you do? My name is Georgina Amelia Whitford Jones. I was just in bed saying my prayers and asking for a friend, preferably Dinesh. I suppose you will do.' She drifted over to a leather armchair and settled into it, her long white nightgown puffing around her. 'Why are you here?'

'I came to find something to eat,' said Lizard, the lie coming easily to him.

'Oh?' Georgina arched a sceptical eyebrow. 'Don't you have a home?'

'I used to live with my uncle, but not anymore. I'll go now,' Lizard said, edging towards the window. 'I'm sorry to disturb you.'

'If you go, I'll scream and scream and scream.' Georgina twirled a lock of her copper hair around her finger.

Lizard stopped.

'Then my maid, Ruksana, will come running and, oh my goodness, the fuss there will be,' said Georgina, eyes wide. She paused to let this sink in. 'Come here, boy.'

Lizard took an unwilling step forward.

Georgina stood up and came closer. She was the same height as Lizard, and he was unnerved when she leaned in, staring at his face. He could smell her breath—sweet and clean. He held his own.

'Your eyes are green,' she said, 'and shaped like a cat's. Your hair is black and your skin is golden.' He flinched when she patted his face. 'You're very pretty, for a boy.'

Abruptly, she whirled round in a flurry of red hair and flounced back to her chair.

Lizard blushed scarlet.

'Tell me your name and where you live and what you do during the day. And,' she stared at him with one eyebrow raised, 'I insist on the truth.'

'They call me Lizard,' he said, reluctantly.

Georgina frowned. 'Why do they call you that?

It's not a very nice name.'

Lizard shrugged. 'My uncle always called me that.'

'And where do you live?'

'I live in Chinatown.'

'So you're a Chinatown lizard?' Georgina's eyes glinted with amusement. 'Where in Chinatown do you live?'

'Above a tailor's shop.' Lizard felt clever for being vague; after all, there were many tailor shops in Chinatown.

'And during the day?'

'Sometimes…I go to school.'

'How can a boy who has to steal food at night pay to go to school during the day?'

Before Lizard could think of a reply, he heard voices outside the front door.

'Oh! They're back much too early!' said Georgina. 'You'll have to hide in the bedroom. Sneak out through the bathroom window when you have a chance.'

Lizard was already dashing into the other room.

'Thank you, Missy,' he said as he dropped down beside one of the beds.

A key turned in the front door and he heard two men speaking in urgent voices outside.

Georgina ducked her head through the bedroom door.

'I haven't finished with you, boy,' she whispered. 'Come back tomorrow night or I shall make sure my father finds you.'

'I can't!' spluttered Lizard, shocked.

'How hard do you think it would be to find a green-eyed half-Chinese boy who lives above a tailor's shop in Chinatown?' She shot him a look of triumph, then turned back to the sitting room as the front door opened.

'Why wasn't I told it was so important, Commander Baxter?' demanded a voice that Lizard recognised as Mr Sebastian Whitford Jones's.

'Well, you know, Navy top brass didn't want too much attention drawn to the thing,' said an unfamiliar voice. 'But never fear, all will be well once you've handed it over.'

'Yes, quite, but nevertheless I ought to have been told of the nature of the thing,' grumbled Mr Whitford Jones.

Lizard moved the mosquito net out of the way and peeped around the bed. The two men stood just inside the front door, with Mrs Whitford Jones behind them. Lizard saw Georgina turn to them.

'Mother? Father?' Her voice trembled. 'Oh, Father, I had the most dreadful nightmare!'

To Lizard's admiration, she burst into loud and believable sobs. He was so impressed that he almost missed her hand waving at him behind her back, just before she pulled the door half closed. She ran and flung herself into her father's arms. Lizard took that as his cue, and he darted to the other end of the bedroom and out the bathroom window.

CHAPTER TWO

Chinatown

Lizard fled down the covered walkway and back into the Palm Court garden. He ducked behind the frangipani tree in the corner and waited while a couple strolled past laughing. The rain had stopped and the damp night air teemed with the sound of crickets chirping, frogs croaking and, in the distance, the Dan Hopkins Orchestra playing a swing tune.

Lizard came to a palm tree next to the garden wall. Making sure there were no Raffles Hotel doormen in sight, Lizard climbed hand-over-hand up the trunk and onto the top of the wall. He crouched there, waiting for a chance to drop unnoticed to the street below. He was very good at climbing and hiding and, he was ashamed to admit, stealing.

Beach Road bustled with activity at this time of

the evening. A few motor cars roared past, taking European gentlemen and their wives to who knows where they went for fun, but mostly the street was full of pedestrians and bicycles and rickshaws pulled by leathery-skinned men with feet as bare as Lizard's own. Beyond the road lay the beachfront and the rhythm of the breaking waves.

Lizard landed on the road and became just another pedestrian in the crowd.

As he walked to Chinatown, he wondered what was in the wooden box. He wanted to open it and see, but not out here where a would-be robber or curious friend might be lurking, sometimes both in the one person. Also, Boss Man Beng had warned him to be extra careful with this particular job.

Lizard needed to pay for rent and food, and he ran errands and did any jobs someone would pay him to do. He did some letter writing on the side too. A lot of his work came from Boss Man Beng.

Boss Man Beng was a petty local criminal who thought of himself as a Chinatown crime boss. In reality, he picked up the crumbs that fell beneath the notice of the big gangs. He had a few spies in Chinatown listening out for information that could be used to make money. Boss Man Beng spent a lot of time sitting in coffee shops talking big, sweating and plotting shady schemes.

Yesterday, Boss Man Beng had called for Lizard, and they had met up at Sum's Coffee Shop.

'Eh, Lizard, this is the big job, really big. Think you can do it?' Boss Man Beng said in Cantonese, a frosty Tiger beer bottle in his hand.

'Do what, Boss?' asked Lizard, his mouth full of the delicious wonton noodles that Boss Man Beng had bought him.

They were sitting at one of the round marble-topped tables in the coffee shop. The sweltering afternoon glare and the rhythmic whirr of the ceiling fan sapped Lizard's energy. Fatty Dim Sum, the proprietor, was humming along to the radio as he wiped the nearby tables.

'I can trust you, eh, Lizard boy? You won't tell anyone?' Boss Man Beng gripped Lizard's shoulder and stared into his eyes. 'You cannot tell anyone or'—his voice dropped to a whisper and he glanced around nervously—'we both could die!'

Lizard was used to Boss Man Beng's exaggerations, but this seemed rather extreme.

'I'll pay you fifty, no, one hundred dollars if you do it right!' Boss Man said.

Lizard had almost choked on his noodles. One hundred dollars! Nearly one year's worth of rent and food. He nodded, swallowed, and said, 'You can trust me, Boss. Whatever you want, I can do it, for sure.'

Boss Man Beng let go of Lizard's shoulder to wipe the sweat off his upper lip. 'All right, boy. You know Raffles Hotel, right? On Beach Road?'

'Yes, Boss. Got a friend who works there, I go there to see him sometimes.'

Boss Man Beng seemed to relax a bit. 'Really? Good, very good. This is what you do...'

After giving Lizard detailed instructions, Boss Man Beng made him repeat them three times before he was satisfied. He took out ten dollars and gave it to Lizard. 'I won't lie to you, boy,' he said, his eyes bulging. 'This is really dangerous. The thing in the teak box is deadly and we need to get rid of it straight away, or…' He drew his index finger across his throat. 'But if things work out,' he grinned fatly, 'I'll get a nice apartment in North Bridge Road and the ladies will…oh, never mind. Just don't be late, understand? Not even one minute, got it?'

Now Lizard had the box and he just needed to give it to Boss Man Beng. But he was unsettled. Not just because the girl Georgina had caught him, but because the way she talked reminded him of Uncle Archie. Lizard forced himself not to think about his uncle when he was on a job—Uncle Archie would be disappointed if he knew Lizard did jobs like this. Being reminded of his uncle so unexpectedly made his chest ache in a way that he couldn't explain.

Lizard walked down North Bridge Road past the Capitol Theatre, one of his favourite places to go when he had any money to spare. He had seen many pictures, but *The Adventures of Robin Hood* was his favourite.

Finally, he turned into Tanjong Pagar Road. This was home now—Chinatown, with its poles of washing hung out of the windows, the fruity stench rising from the open drains on the sides of the road and the clamour of hawkers hustling in their dialects. The upper floors of the shop houses jutted out over the street, forming a covered walkway along the roadside. Sir Stamford Raffles had decreed that this walkway be five foot wide, and everyone called it the five-foot way.

Lizard realised he was ravenous.

'Eh, Lizard! You so late tonight? What you doing?' the Indian hawker was already taking out the curry puffs as he spoke.

'Eh, uncle, how?' he greeted the hawker. The hawker was not actual family, but *uncle* was the respectful way to address any older man, even strangers. Curry puffs were Lizard's favourite food, and he always silently dedicated the first bite to Uncle Archie. He could usually only afford two once a week, but today, he could have as many as he wanted.

'I'm very good, yes,' said the hawker.

As Lizard sat down at a wooden stool in front of the curry-puff cart, he thought about Georgina

Whitford Jones and what she had said about him sounding like her. He certainly didn't sound like her when he was speaking to anyone in Tanjong Pagar Road.

'Here comes tailor Missy for her weekly curry puffs,' said the hawker.

Lizard looked up with a mouth full of pastry and saw his best friend, Lili, walking towards him. Lili's father Mr Mak had the tailor shop above which Lizard lived.

'*Wei*, *Lili*, *deem ah*?' he greeted her in Cantonese and drew the back of his hand across his mouth to wipe off the pastry flakes.

'*Aiyoh*, Lizard,' she replied. 'You know my teacher told me to practise English. Speak dialect at home only.'

'Huh?' said Lizard. 'I don't have a home.'

'What do you mean?' said Lili, perching herself on a stool next to Lizard. 'We live in the same place.'

Lizard thought about the bunk-sized cubicle he rented above Lili's father's shop. All his few belongings were crammed in his tiny space, which was separated from those on either side of him by thin partitions. Sixteen other people lived on the same floor, including a family of five in the front room.

Lili lived downstairs with her family, which had only six people, plus a servant girl. She used to have a little brother, but he'd died of cholera when he was two. Lili's family had three proper bedrooms, a kitchen, a living room, an open air light well and a back courtyard. Her father's tailor's shop at the front was the only part Lizard had seen.

'No, we don't live in the same place at all,' said Lizard with a grin. 'Watch out, your brother is coming. Don't talk to me or he'll tell your father.'

Lili quickly stood up and turned her back to Lizard.

'Twenty curry puffs please, uncle,' she said to the grinning hawker. 'Hello, *Dai Goh*,' she said to her brother.

'Father says hurry up with the curry puffs,' said her elder brother as he walked past. He lifted his chin at Lizard in acknowledgment and carried on down the road.

Lili watched him walk away before sitting down again. They had never discussed it, but Lizard knew that Lili's whole family would disapprove of her friendship with him. Lili was fully Chinese; Lizard wasn't. Lili had a family; Lizard didn't. Lili wasn't dirt poor; Lizard was.

'What have you got in your dirty old bag?' she asked Lizard.

'Nothing!' he said. All in a rush, he remembered his errand and jumped off the stool, clutching the satchel tight. 'I have to go. Bye!'

Lili watched him hurry off as the hawker handed her the curry puffs. She wanted to ask where he was going, but she was careful never to question him too closely. After all, she had secrets of her own to keep.

Lizard arrived at the Singapore Railway Station in Keppel Road at 9pm. He was to meet Boss Man Beng under the station clock at exactly 10pm, so he had an hour to kill.

He had followed all of Boss Man Beng's instructions from yesterday afternoon, and now the only thing left was to hand the teak box over to him and collect his ninety dollars, since he had got the first ten before the job. Ten dollars was already more money than Lizard had ever had at one time.

Boss Man Beng had said not to be late, not even one minute. Lizard squatted against the wall under the station clock, the satchel pulled in close. People hurried past: the women in saris, samfoos, dresses or hijabs; the men in singlets, suits, sarongs or turbans. Lizard yawned and thought about the Chinatown boys gambling in Smith Street, as they did every night. It was going to be a boring hour, squatting here. He stood up. It wasn't far to Smith Street, and he could be back by 10 o'clock, no problem.

Lizard hurried off to find the boys.

There they were, scrawny lads in singlets and cotton shorts crowded around a rickety table, with a lantern strung up above them. Raucous jokes and happy insults were traded in a mash of Chinese dialects with smatterings of Malay and Indian words. On the table was a little wooden box and some dice. The boys put out piles of coins and placed bets.

Ah Ling and Ah Keung greeted Lizard with cheerful punches on his upper arm and made a space for him at the table.

There were three or four older lads Lizard didn't recognise. He hoped there wouldn't be trouble. One of the big boys was taller than the others and his hair was slicked back with Brylcreem. You could see the grooves a comb had tracked though his gleaming hair. He lounged against a concrete pillar, looked down into Lizard's face and gave a slow, mean grin.

There was going to be trouble.

'Half-half boy,' drawled the Brylcreem lad in Hokkien. Lizard glanced up and around, noting the overhang of the five-foot way, the concrete posts on either side, the wooden crates lying nearby and, as always, the uncovered monsoon drain at the roadside.

Ah Ling and Ah Keung were his friends, but they grinned too and moved back. They wanted to see some fun. The other boys grabbed their money, the little box and the dice off the table and also backed up.

'What you doing here, half-half boy?' asked another big lad, following the leader. This one had buck teeth. 'This place is for Chinese boys only.'

'Maybe you some part Chinese, ah?' said Brylcreem. 'Tell you what, boy, your Chinese part can stay. The rest, get lost.' He guffawed and elbowed Buck Tooth in the ribs.

That was a new one, Lizard had to admit. He couldn't afford any trouble, not tonight. Boss Man Beng's sweaty face warning him not to be late flashed in front of his eyes.

'Hey, no problem, I'll go, I'll go,' Lizard said in Hokkien. He put his hand on his satchel to make sure the box was safely there.

Brylcreem wasn't stupid. His cunning eyes darted to the cotton bag. 'What you got there, huh? A present for me?'

Lizard took a step back. He couldn't lose the box, and he couldn't be late to meet Boss Man Beng. It was stupid to have come here. How much time had passed? Lizard couldn't be sure.

Brylcreem advanced and made a grab for the bag. He yanked it hard, and Lizard cannoned into him, his head whacking Brylcreem in the eye.

'*Ow!*' Brylcreem yelled. He clapped a hand to his right eye. Hokkien swear words peppered the humid night air. He punched Lizard hard in the mouth.

The punch took Lizard by surprise, and he tasted the metal tang of blood.

'*Alamak!*' Lizard put all his frustration into the Malay exclamation, then he leapt up, pushed himself against a concrete post and grabbed the overhang of the five-foot way. He hung there for a moment, his satchel still safely around his neck. Buck Tooth lurched out to hit him, but Lizard bent his knees up to his chest and Buck Tooth missed. Then Lizard dropped his feet and thumped his heels into Buck Tooth's back, pushing him into the rickety table, which tipped over with a clatter.

Around them, the younger boys congratulated each other on their wisdom in taking their stuff off that table.

Brylcreem staggered towards Lizard, swearing furiously, and, with careful aim, Lizard swung his legs and propelled him into the open drain at the side of the road. The other boys leapt back to avoid the foul splash.

Lizard hoisted himself up to the first floor. Boss Man's words rang in his ears: *Don't be late, not even one minute.* He shinnied down the post and hit the street running, clutching the satchel. He didn't need to look back to know that the younger boys would have set up the table again and placed their bets before he reached the end of the road.

Lizard kept running until he could see the railway station clock. He was not one but ten minutes late for his meeting with Boss Man Beng.

There was a commotion outside the station. He couldn't see Boss Man Beng. A dense crowd pushed and shouted right under the station clock. Lizard frowned; how was he going to find the Boss in that uproar?

'What's happening?' he asked a boy at the edge of the crowd.

The boy spun round to face him. 'Somebody got stabbed there, just now! Stabbed!'

'What?' said Lizard, with a jolt of shock. 'Who? How?'

The boy shrugged. 'Some man, don't know who.'

Lizard shoved and squeezed his way through the crowd, dread growing in his belly. Finally, he broke through to the centre and found himself staring into the contorted face of Boss Man Beng. He was lying on his back. A knife was stuck in his chest and blood welled out, soaking his shirt and pooling on the ground.

'Boss!' Lizard cried, dropping to his knees.

Boss Man Beng's bulging eyes looked at him. His lips were moving, and his hand clawed at Lizard's.

Lizard grabbed Boss Man's hand and leaned forward to listen, but he couldn't hear anything over the pandemonium around him. When Boss Man's lips stopped moving, Lizard gazed desperately at his face, but the man's stare became fixed and unseeing. And when the grip of his hand went slack, Lizard knew that he was dead, and that he would never know what the Boss had been trying to tell him.

Lizard knelt in the pool of blood holding Boss Man's hand, wishing he could wake up from this ghastly, freakish nightmare.

CHAPTER THREE

The Box of Bad Luck

This couldn't be possible. Any second now, Boss Man Beng would get up and laugh at him. Lizard blinked to wake himself up. Then, as it sank in that the Boss really was dead, his heart galloped so loud that he couldn't hear anything else, and he breathed so fast that he felt lightheaded.

Lizard was familiar with death. Chinatown people were hardy, until they weren't. Typhoid, cholera, dysentery and accidents were sudden; tuberculosis was slower, with more coughing. Sago Lane, near where Lizard lived, was famous for its death houses. Death happened, but it had never happened like this—right in front of him—to someone he knew.

When his brain started working again, his first thought was, 'But I didn't tell anyone!'

His second thought was, 'And I'm not dead!'

His third thought was, 'Yet.'

Boss Man had said that the box was dangerous and if things went wrong they could both die. Things had definitely gone wrong—Boss Man was dead and Lizard would be next.

Lizard turned and shoved his way blindly back through the crowd of yelling, ogling people. As he emerged, he heard a policeman's whistle in the distance. There was nothing he could do for Boss Man Beng now, but he could do his best to keep himself alive. Terror squirted through his arteries with every heartbeat.

His instinct was to run, but he slowed his steps. He didn't want to draw attention to himself. He missed Uncle Archie more than ever. Uncle Archie would have known what to do.

Lizard's mother had sent him to live in a stilt house by the sea in Changi with Uncle Archie, his dead father's brother, when he was four years old. He remembered his mother kissing him goodbye, and then the amah taking him on a long bus ride that night. The next morning he'd woken up in a strange bed, and a surprised-looking man with a pointy nose and blue-grey eyes was hovering over him. Lizard had never seen eyes that colour before—his mother was Cantonese and everybody in his world up until then had been Chinese or Malay or Indian. He thought everyone but him had brown eyes.

Uncle Archie had sat next to him, opened a blue envelope and taken a long time to read the letter. After that, he'd seemed to accept that he had to take care of Lizard, just because Lizard was his nephew, even though he'd never met Lizard before and had needed lots of help to look after him. After all, what did an unmarried thirty-year-old British man know about four-year-old children?

When Lizard asked when he was returning to his mother, Uncle Archie would clear his throat and say she had to go away and he didn't know when she would be back. As the years went by, Lizard had stopped asking, though the hurt of being given away like a bundle of rags had never fully gone away.

Pak Tuah, the headman of the Malay fishing village west of their stilt house, had helped Uncle Archie look after Lizard, and Lizard had grown up fishing and swimming and playing with the kids in the Malay village. Pak Tuah's children, Zikri and Aminah, had given him the nickname of Lizard, because his initials were LZD and he climbed trees like a lizard.

He learned Chinese and mathematics from Teacher Foon in the Chinese village nearby, and Uncle Archie taught him English, history and geography in a haphazard fashion. There was also a scouting manual that Lizard and his uncle both loved. Lizard remembered afternoons on the verandah where Uncle Archie would toss his sun-lightened hair out of his eyes and show Lizard how to tie the 'knot of the week'.

Uncle Archie told everyone he was a writer, but Lizard never saw much writing being done. He wondered what Uncle Archie did all day, so he followed him once. His uncle had grabbed his dark blue trilby from the selection of hats by the door and gone out. Lizard tailed him all the way to the Changi Military Base, but he couldn't go in without being seen. He knew Uncle Archie had been in the British Navy so he figured he was visiting old friends.

Sometimes, Uncle Archie had to go away for days—'to the city'—or even for weeks—'hunting'— and Lizard would stay with Pak Tuah's family.

Lizard was ten years old when he last saw his uncle. He never forgot the last words Uncle Archie had said to him, before he vanished. 'Lizard, old chap, I've got to go to the city today, but I'll be back this evening. What do you say to Chinatown curry puffs for supper?'

Of course, Lizard had agreed—he loved curry puffs. He hadn't even hugged his uncle goodbye as he dashed out the door, scared to be late for strict Teacher Foon. But Uncle Archie hadn't come back that evening. Lizard had taken the dark blue trilby to bed and slept with it on as the rain clattered all night long on the tin roof.

He'd stayed at Pak Tuah's, and Pak Tuah tried to find Uncle Archie, but there was no trace. One day,

Lizard had gone back to the stilt house and found it ransacked—table overturned, books and dishes on the floor, cupboard doors open. He wandered around in shock. Something had happened to Uncle Archie, he knew it, and Pak Tuah wasn't going to find him. Lizard picked up a photo of Uncle Archie off the floor and tucked it into his pocket.

He would have to find Uncle Archie himself. Not here and not in any Changi village. Uncle Archie had gone to the city—that's where Lizard would have to look for him. Pak Tuah would never let Lizard go to the city and it would be rude to disobey him. It would be better to just go without asking. As he left, Lizard grabbed his uncle's trilby and put it on his head.

He took the mosquito bus to the city and looked everywhere for Uncle Archie, but hadn't found him. No one would help him. He'd ended up in Chinatown where the local boys doled out jeers and knocks because he was new, odd looking and had no clan to belong to. He stayed alive on the erratic kindness of the shopkeepers and by running errands.

Always in his heart was the hope of finding Uncle Archie, and always in his mind was the expectation that Uncle Archie would come home with curry puffs to share.

Life had been a struggle until he had met Lili.

As he walked back to the home Lili had organised for him, Lizard kept saying to himself: 'Walk slow. Be calm. Be safe.' Policemen in khaki uniforms ran past and Lizard kept his head down, making sure not to look.

Boss Man Beng was so very dead now, and Lizard wished he could ask Uncle Archie what to do. As if he'd called him up through sheer desperation, Uncle Archie's voice sounded in his ears, a verse Lizard had often heard him recite: 'Always remember, Lizard, when things start going down the drain, think once, think twice, then think again.'

Lizard took a deep breath and forced himself to think. He was sure that Boss Man Beng had been killed because of the teak box from Raffles Hotel. That must mean somebody badly wanted the box. If they knew that he, Lizard, had it, then he would be dead too. So whoever killed Boss Man Beng didn't know that Lizard had the box. As long as he kept calm and didn't give himself away, he would be safe.

Lizard went to rub his eyes and noticed that his hand was clenched. He was holding something— some sort of cloth, scrunched up. Boss Man Beng must have had it in his hand when he grabbed Lizard's. Lizard shuddered as he saw that there was blood on it, and he shoved it into his satchel.

When Lizard arrived at Mak's Tailor Shop, he nearly cried with relief. The building hadn't ever felt like home before, but it felt that way now. It was even better when he saw Lili sitting on a small stool outside the shop. She was reading by the light of an oil lamp on a crate beside her. The metal lattice security grills of the shop had been pulled nearly closed, and the lights in the shop had been dimmed. Lizard walked up to her, making sure to stand where he couldn't be seen by Mr Mak, in case he looked out.

Lili gasped when she saw him. She jumped up and stared at his face. 'Lizard!' she exclaimed. 'What happened to you?'

Lizard didn't know where to start, or even whether he should start. All he could do was look at Lili's comforting, familiar, heart-shaped face.

She put out a hand and touched his jaw with gentle fingers and clicked her tongue. 'Did you fight again?' she asked.

He opened his mouth, then closed it and nodded. Only then did he feel the throbbing pain of his swollen, split lip.

'Did they call you names again?'

He shrugged.

Lili sighed. She pulled her small stool further from the shop's doorway and motioned for him to sit down. 'Wait here,' she said, and she ducked inside.

Lizard sat down, then he moved himself and the stool even further into the shadows. Metal security grills clashed shut across shopfronts up and down the road. All around him, the inhabitants of Tanjong Pagar Road were settling into their night-time routines. The familiarity was soothing, and he felt himself relax.

The Sikh nightwatchman for the tobacco factory two doors down was climbing into the string bed he put across the entrance every night. Lizard heard him spit the last paan juice of the day into the drain nearby. Weary hawkers plodded past, pushing their carts home.

Lili reappeared next to him, and he jumped.

'Are you all right, Lizard?' she asked, with a little frown.

Lizard nodded.

She handed him a cup. 'Ovaltine. Not too hot,' she said and she pressed a cold, wet cloth gently to his lip.

Lizard started with the pain.

'Hold it there when you're not drinking,' Lili said.

Lizard took a sip of the Ovaltine, wincing as the cup touched his lip. The warm, sweet liquid was the best thing he had ever tasted. Lili put the lamp on the ground and pulled the crate closer to Lizard. As she sat down, her hair fell forward.

'Your hair is so straight and shiny and black,' Lizard said dreamily.

Lili's eyebrows shot up.

'Have you ever seen red hair? A little gold, but mostly red? Shiny, wavy, red-gold hair.' Lizard took another swallow of Ovaltine. 'Red hair is very pretty. And blue eyes. Blue eyes are pretty too.'

Lili stared at him.

Lizard continued to gaze vaguely into space.

Lili jumped up. 'Finished?' she snapped. Then she grabbed the cup, spilling the last of the Ovaltine.

'What? No, I...' Lizard mumbled, startled.

Lili turned on her heel and vanished into the shop, and the grills slammed shut behind her.

Lizard was left holding the damp cloth to his mouth. 'What did I say?' he asked the empty air where Lili had been a moment ago.

He tucked the stool behind the crate and picked up the lamp that Lili had forgotten to take with her. It would come in useful tonight. He wanted to see what was in the teak box that was so important a man had been killed for it. He was sad for Boss Man Beng, and worried, but lurking at the back of his mind was the regret of ninety dollars that he was never going to get.

Lizard made his way up the narrow wooden steps to the landing. A couple of knee-high kids ran past him, yelling at each other in Cantonese. He could hear the clash of metal against a wok as someone fried up their garlicky supper in the sooty communal kitchen. Nobody paid him any attention as he went down the narrow corridor to his dark, stuffy cubicle.

He kept his tiny home as neat as he could. There was a shelf above his bed for his bowl, chopsticks and spoon. The dark blue trilby hat hung from a nail on the wall. On the nail next to it hung his school clothes. If you didn't keep things orderly in tropical Singapore, vermin and decay soon ruined them. His other meagre belongings were stacked under his bed.

Lizard sat on his bed, put the lamp on the floor and hung the damp cloth Lili had given him on the edge of his shelf. There were electric lights in the building, but they had cheap, low-powered light bulbs in them and there wasn't one in his cubicle. He took the satchel off—finally!— and dumped it on his bed with a shrug to loosen his shoulders.

Now to see what was in the box.

'*Wei*, Lizard.'

Lizard looked up with a sigh. 'What, Ah Mok?' he asked in Cantonese.

'*Wah*, why your mouth all swell up?' Ah Mok lived in the next cubicle. He waved a hand at Lizard's face.

'Never mind,' Lizard grunted.

'All right. Hey, I've got another customer for you.' The boy grinned proudly at Lizard.

'Maybe tomorrow. I'm busy,' Lizard said, glancing at the satchel on his bed.

'He waiting outside! He got money now! Five cents for you, five cents for me!'

Lizard looked at the scrawny boy's pleading face. With five cents Ah Mok could buy an egg with his rice for lunch tomorrow.

'All right. Go get him.' Lizard reached under his bunk and took out a large tin box. It used to hold Huntley and Palmers soda crackers but that was a long time ago. He took the lid off and lifted out his ink, brush and water jar. His paper was running low—he would need to get more.

Ah Mok came back with a coolie from Collyer Quay. He was a gnarled brown branch of a man who looked sixty but was probably thirty.

The man squinted suspiciously at Lizard. 'Can write Chinese, ah? And so young...' he said in a thick village Cantonese accent. He squatted on his haunches and dictated a letter to his wife in China. Lizard transformed his words into legible, if not particularly elegant, brush strokes. The man waited each time Lizard consulted his prized and battered dictionary. Finally, they were done.

'Remember, it's our little secret,' Ah Mok said to the man as they left the cubicle. 'Don't tell anybody or the real letter writers will put us out of business.'

Lizard stashed his writing things back under the bed.

'See,' said Ah Mok, tossing a coin to Lizard as he came back into the cubicle. 'Good idea, right? We can use your high-class schooling to make money.'

'We're in trouble if the letter writers find out.' Lizard said, and he flopped down on his bed, exhausted.

'No, no, the worst maybe we have to give them protection money,' said Ah Mok in a soothing tone.

'No, the worst is the real letter writers pay a gang to kill us,' Lizard said gloomily, death being very much on his mind. 'They wouldn't bother with the death houses in Sago Lane—they'd just drop us in a drain. Go away, Ah Mok.'

Ah Mok shrugged and did as he was told, happily flipping his five-cent coin in the air as he went.

Lizard wondered if his Chinese teacher at St Andrew's Mission School would be disappointed if she knew that he was using calligraphy skills to make money like this. At least it was practical experience. No, he thought, the letter writing wasn't wrong—not like the stealing.

Lizard waited until he was certain that everybody around him was asleep before he turned up the lamp and took the teak box out of his satchel. He rested it on his lap and ran his fingers over the smooth, dark wood. The box had brass hinges and a brass catch, which was held together by a metal ring that had been soldered shut. He pulled on the ring. It felt pretty solid. Someone had taken a lot of trouble to stop anyone opening it. Now Lizard wanted even more to know what was inside.

He couldn't open the box—or could he? Grabbing his satchel, he slung it on and put the box in it. He turned the lamp down low and picked it up. All was dark and quiet in the building as he padded to the communal kitchen and found what he was looking for. Next to the brazier, secure in its folded newspaper sheath, was a heavy Chinese chopper. The metal ring on the box felt solid but Lizard was sure the chopper would win out. He sneaked out the back door, down the spiral staircase and into the back alley below.

It was still noisy outside even at this time of night, with dogs barking, cats wailing, men stumbling home from opium dens, or still gambling and laughing and arguing and cooking and eating and hawking and spitting. From somewhere nearby, Lizard could hear the clatter of mah-jong tiles being expertly swirled as raucous Hokkien grandmothers gossiped and wagered their way through the sticky, sultry night.

He put the lamp on the ground and turned it up.

Then he took the box out of his satchel and arranged it so that the ring lay against a concrete step. He unsheathed the chopper and gave the ring a small whack. When there was absolutely no change to the night sounds around him, he took heart and began chopping at the ring with force. The rhythmic clank added to the night's music.

On the seventh whack, the ring split apart. Lizard grinned and wiped the sweat off his brow with the back of his forearm. He was careful to re-sheathe the chopper. A Chinese chopper always gets respect.

He sat down and opened the box. Inside was a package wrapped in brown waxed paper and tied with string. Was it safer to open the package here in the alley or back in his cubicle? A familiar stink and the sound of buckets clonking from down the lane made his mind up for him. It was the night soil man, coming to change the full toilet buckets for empty ones all along the night soil ports of the back lane.

Lizard slammed the box lid shut, shoved the box back into his satchel and hurried up the spiral stairs.

Back in his cubicle, he put the lamp on the floor,

sat on his bunk and took out the box. The string was tied in a knot he knew well: the Zeppelin bend. His breath caught in his throat as he felt the string and found that it wasn't string at all but parachute cord. The Zeppelin bend was one of the knots Uncle Archie had taught him to tie, and parachute cord was what Uncle Archie always used. Lizard brought the lamp closer. The cord was made of braided coloured strands: red, white and blue—exactly the same as the cord Uncle Archie used.

Lizard's heart squeezed tight as he stared at the knot. It was as if his uncle had sent a message to him.

Now he really needed to know what was inside. He untied the knot and unwrapped the stiff brown paper. Inside was a book of some sort. Lizard brought it closer to the lamp and flipped through the pages. The whole thing was filled with columns of five-digit numbers alongside columns of Chinese— no, Japanese—characters. It was the type of script he had seen on the Japanese shops in Middle Road.

Maybe it was a textbook for teaching mathematics to Japanese children. But surely nobody would kill a man for a textbook. What could this book possibly be? All Lizard knew was that the book meant trouble, whatever it was. The thought of going to the authorities crossed his mind, but only for a moment.

The British owned and ran Singapore, or at least everyone let them think that they did. The British authorities didn't understand anything and mostly didn't care, as long as their house boys served the tea on time.

Lizard carefully wrapped the book back in the waxed paper and tied it up again with a Zeppelin knot.

The box haunted Lizard. Since it had come into his life, just a few hours ago, he had been caught stealing, been beaten up, seen Boss Man Beng murdered and made Lili mad at him. Lizard feared the box, but he also burned with curiosity. What was the book, and what was it for? And could it have something to do with his uncle's disappearance?

Lizard had to find out. He would go back to where he had got it—Raffles Hotel. His uncle had taught him scouting skills, and now he was going to use them. Also, he hadn't forgotten the beautiful, yet horribly pushy Georgina Whitford Jones and her threat to set her father looking for him if he didn't return.

Lizard lay on his bunk, staring at a small, pale gecko on the underside of his shelf. It was missing its tail. It must have lost it in some sort of struggle. The tail would grow back, he knew, but it would never be the same as before.

He turned his head and touched the sepia photo of his smiling uncle in uniform pinned up on the wall by his bed. 'Goodnight, Uncle Archie. Wherever you are,' he said.

CHAPTER FOUR

The Mission

'Uh!' Lili grunted as she kicked open the locked door. A quick forward roll brought her into the middle of the room. She crouched, knife poised, as she swept the place with a glance. One window, open. A bulky man, sitting at a table strewn with papers. A meat safe, its doors open, showing stacks of plates and bowls inside. A wok to the left. A sack of rice on the floor.

The man stood up, wielding his own knife. Lili exploded from her crouch and kicked his stomach. As he doubled over, her other foot smacked against his temple and he collapsed.

Lili sheathed her knife and dashed to the meat safe. She yanked the stacks of plates and bowls and sent them crashing to the floor. Then she gathered all the papers on the table, rolled them up and shoved them into a deep pocket in the front of her tunic.

With a grin, she turned to leave. She was certain that Lizard's red-haired girl couldn't down a man and acquire top-secret plans like she just had. But before she reached the door there was a pattering noise behind her and something whacked her hard in the back. She sprawled to the floor. Instinctively, she dodged, and a boot stomped right where her head had been a split second ago. Lili glanced up at her opponent, who was dressed just like her, all in black and wearing a face mask.

She pushed up into a charge straight at her assailant, who sidestepped with a mocking snort and helped Lili on her way into the wall with a two-handed shove.

Lili crashed head first into the wall and crumpled. Her opponent grabbed her shoulder, spun her around and reached into the front of her tunic to seize the papers. The black-clad figure then drew back and delivered a swift spear-hand thrust into Lili's stomach.

'Ha!' Lili thought triumphantly as her adversary's

fingertips hit the metal plate she wore tucked under her tunic.

Her opponent bent over with an agonised groan.

Lili sat up, grabbed the papers and drew back to deliver an almighty punch.

'Stop!' yelled Miss Adelia. 'Exercise over.'

Lili dropped the papers and took her mask off, glad to get her sweaty face back into fresh air. Mr Bee, the bulky man, got up off the floor, lifted the padded helmet off his head and limped towards the other two. He pulled off Lili's opponent's mask.

'Aw, Ying, what's happened here?' he asked in a broad New Zealand accent. Everyone called him Mr Bee—Lili didn't know whether that was his actual surname, the initial of his surname, or a code name. Ying didn't answer him. She just stared at Lili, her eyebrows pulled down in an angry V-shape.

Ying held up her right hand. The index and ring fingers were oddly bent.

'Broken, I'd say. Two fingers broken!' said Mr Bee.

Miss Adelia's face was creased with frowning.

She had bobbed hair that was silver in colour but a face that was young and usually unlined.

'What happened, Lili?' she snapped.

Lili gulped, reached into her tunic and pulled out the small tin plate, hammered to fit snugly over her solar plexus.

Miss Adelia's lips flattened ominously. 'Explanation, please.'

'The sisters said to watch out for Ying. Her new move, the spear-hand thrust, made them feel like they'd never be able to breathe again, so I've been wearing this under my combat tunic ever since.'

Lili saw the two scowling sisters Yun Meng and Yun Lai leaning through the window and well within earshot. Lili had managed to offend all her S-Stream classmates in two minutes.

'Right, then. I'll take Ying down to the nurse,' said Mr Bee. 'Looks like we'll have to call the doctor again.' Ying glared at Lili as she left.

'Whatever possessed you, Lili?' Miss Adelia said. 'I need Ying in perfect condition for a mission.' She closed her mouth with a snap. 'Come with me.'

Lili followed her out of the house into a wide, airy gymnasium. The house they had just left was fake. It could be set up to suit whatever training situation was required by Maximum Operations Enterprise, an intelligence organisation funded by the British government.

A few years ago, Miss Adelia and her superior, Miss Neha, had pushed for the training of local children as spies, and the result was the top secret S-Stream Program, which was based at an all girls' school. There were four girls in the training program: Lili and Ying and sisters Yun Meng and Yun Lai.

All the other schoolgirls knew that the four S-Stream pupils were gifted and in a special class (the S in S-Stream stood for Special). What they didn't know was that they were also learning to be spies for the British Empire.

Miss Adelia waved at Lili to take a seat at the table in front of the fake house and dismissed the sisters—one of whom had a bandaged ankle and the other a bandaged knee. They limped out, scowling.

'What were you thinking?' Miss Adelia's silver hair crackled with angry energy.

Lili wondered once again how old Miss Adelia was. She guessed at twenty-eight, or maybe thirty. She had heard that English women didn't like to tell their age so she'd never asked.

'I was tired of Ying hurting us!' Lili said. 'She always wins the training fights, and we end up in pain, so when the sisters told me about her new spear-hand thrust—'

'Ying always wins because she works hard. But she is also careful not to seriously hurt any of you. Your clever stunt has created a big problem. We had plans for Ying—'

'But I found the papers!' said Lili. 'That was today's mission, and I found the papers!'

'No, you didn't,' Miss Adelia said. 'More plans were taped behind the meat safe. Your search was not systematic, and you didn't see that Ying was hiding in the rice sack. That was unacceptably careless. And noisy! Maximum Operations agents are stealthy. No smashing crockery. It's a fact-gathering mission, Lili, not a Greek wedding.' Miss Adelia's shrewd hazel eyes assessed her. 'What happened?'

Lili shrugged, red-faced.

'You must focus and not be distracted. Maximum Operations Enterprise is the best intelligence organisation in the British Empire. The Empire is already at war with Nazi Germany. And war is brewing all over the world, even here in Singapore. You will need all your training if you are to be useful to Maximum Ops.'

Lili nodded, her face burning. Behind the meat safe? So easy, and she had missed them. Miss Adelia was right—she had been distracted, by Lizard, by red hair and by her envy of Ying.

'Well, Yun Meng and Yun Lai are also injured, so it looks like you'll be taking this job.' The gym doors opened. 'Here comes Miss Neha now with the mission brief.'

Lili was excited to be getting her first real mission, but she felt guilty at robbing Ying of her chance.

An elegant lady in her thirties wearing a pink sari approached, carrying a briefcase in one hand. School rumour was that Miss Neha was a rebellious princess of an Indian princely state who had run away in her youth.

She put the briefcase on the table and looked around. 'Good, no chance of being overheard,' she said. 'Everything in order, Miss Adelia?'

'Actually, I need a word.' Miss Adelia drew her aside and spoke in a low voice.

Lili strained her ears and caught a few words. 'Ying...fingers broken...can't possibly...' Miss Adelia waved her hands. '*Both* sisters hurt...'

The two ladies headed back to the table. 'Well, we have to do our best. I am sure Lili is up to the task,' said Miss Neha.

'As long as she isn't distracted,' said Miss Adelia, looking straight at Lili.

'Please, give me a chance!' Lili exclaimed, then sat back and composed herself. 'I won't lose concentration again.'

'I hope that's true, Lili,' said Miss Adelia. 'Carry on, Miss Neha.'

'Your first assignment takes place this evening.

We need an agent who won't be noticed. As we know, nobody notices girls.' Miss Neha opened the briefcase, took out a world map and spread it out on the table. She tapped China. 'The Japanese Empire is expanding from war in China and spreading south, towards us. Malaya and Singapore are in great danger.'

'The British are not pleased. Our bases here and in Malaya must be protected,' Miss Adelia said grimly. 'The gunjin leave a trail of utter devastation.'

Lili nodded. The gunjin—the Japanese military—had shocked everyone with their brutal treatment of the Chinese, starting when they invaded Shanghai in 1937. She had once overheard her stepmother telling a neighbour in shocked tones about how even the children in one village had been killed by the soldiers, but Lili couldn't believe anybody could do something so terrible.

'The Japanese want to take over Singapore,' said Miss Neha. A shiver went up Lili's spine at the thought of gunjin in Singapore. She would do everything she could to help stop that from happening.

Lili thought about the portrait of Emperor Hirohito of Japan and the portrait of King George VI of the British Empire. Both were men in medal-laden military uniforms. Both were determined to have Singapore.

'Japan has joined forces with Nazi Germany, which is bad news for us,' said Miss Adelia.

Lili looked at the two women, wondering what missions they had completed in the field. She had always thought of them as teachers, not spies, but of course they were both.

'What must I do?' Lili asked.

'There is a very important box that must be found,' said Miss Adelia. 'Do you remember the codebreaking lesson on book ciphers?'

'Yes,' said Lili. 'The sender writes a message, then uses a codebook to replace the words with numbers or other letters.'

'Yes,' said Miss Adelia. 'The receiver must also have a codebook, in order to decipher the message. Lili, this mission is top secret. You must tell no one—not even the other S-Stream girls. Understand?'

Lili nodded, eyes wide.

'A Japanese Navy codebook was put in a wooden box and smuggled out of China by one of our Maximum Ops agents,' said Miss Neha. 'This codebook is extremely important—if we have it, the War Office in England will be able to decode messages that the Japanese Navy send to each other. If they plan to attack a British territory, we'll be able to intercept before it happens.'

'The Japanese Navy uses book ciphers,' said Miss Neha. 'This one codes a word or phrase into a five-digit number. For example, the word 'aerodrome' might be the number 20948. The War Office has managed to break some of the code but it's hard, slow work.'

'Wars are won on information, Lili. This codebook is absolutely crucial. We must get it back,' Miss Adelia said.

Maybe Lili's mission could stop the gunjin coming to Singapore—if she succeeded. She *had* to succeed.

'Great Britain is not at war with Japan, and we

hope to avoid war,' said Miss Adelia. 'If the codebook is found in British military hands we fear that the situation will worsen.'

'The Maximum Ops agent was captured by the gunjin, but he managed to get the box away before they knew he had it. The box was given to Sebastian Whitford Jones, the general manager of the New British East India Company. He was to take the box into Singapore and give it to the British Navy.' Miss Neha paused. 'Unfortunately, the box has been stolen from Mr Whitford Jones.'

Miss Adelia snorted. 'All he had to do was bring it from New Delhi and give it to Commander Baxter. A few hours in Singapore, and he loses it.'

'The box was removed from his suite in Raffles Hotel sometime yesterday,' said Miss Neha.

'We must have that codebook if we are to defend ourselves against Japan,' said Miss Adelia.

'But you said we are not at war with Japan,' said Lili, confused.

'Well, not yet,' said Miss Adelia. 'We must be ready in case it happens.'

Lili didn't understand why countries wanted war—why couldn't everyone just get along? But war was a reality, and that was why Maximum Operations Enterprise was necessary.

Miss Neha opened a file. 'We've received information about Mr Whitford Jones that makes us wonder if he is playing us false. He's quite heavily in debt. It's possible that he has taken the codebook to sell back to the Japanese.'

'We don't know for sure that Mr Whitford Jones is selling us out, but we need to put him under surveillance,' said Miss Adelia. 'Your mission is to go to Raffles Hotel to observe him. Is he secretly passing packages to Japanese agents? Having secret meetings? You must take the Minox camera and plenty of film. Photograph anyone he meets.'

Miss Neha handed Lili a folder. 'This file contains photographs of Sebastian Whitford Jones and his family, diagrams of Raffles Hotel, a list of staff and guests, and further instructions. We'll need a full written mission report afterwards.'

Lili clutched the folder, thrilled. After three

years of training, she had been given her first mission at last!

Later that day, Lili stood in the equipment room. Everything she took for her mission had to fit into her special tunic and trousers. The outfit had many hidden pockets, yet looked like something any Chinese girl would wear. The miniature camera, plus a handful of film canisters, were the first things she picked up. Her hand hovered over the lock-picking set, but this was just a surveillance mission, so she left it and took a miniature spyglass instead. She also picked up a sleep dart, and strapped a wrist dagger securely in place inside her sleeve. Just in case. As she smoothed down her tunic, she knew that the most important thing was not to bungle her first Max Ops solo mission, or be distracted, especially not by Lizard.

She thought about what Lizard had said last night. After all she had done for him in the two years since they met, what thanks had she got? He had certainly never gazed into space while mumbling about her eyes and hair. *Red* hair! *Blue* eyes! Where had he seen those close enough to be so fascinated by them?

She remembered the first time she had seen Lizard in the Tanjong Pagar wet market. She'd gone there with her older cousin Ting Ha to buy vegetables. Ting Ha had yelled out in Cantonese and Lili turned to see her holding a skinny boy by the wrist. He had tried to pick Ting Ha's pocket, but hadn't been very good at it. When Lili got closer, she noticed the boy's green eyes. He apologised and tried to get away, but Ting Ha had a firm grip.

Lili had been fascinated that this green-eyed boy could speak Cantonese. He told Ting Ha that he'd tried to pick her pocket because he was hungry. Something about him made Lili think of her baby brother who had died the year before. Then Lizard had looked at Lili, and to her own surprise she made Ting Ha let him go and then went to buy him some kway teow. The fried rice-noodle dish was the most fattening thing she could think of.

She watched him eat, and then, when his

chopsticks slowed down, she figured it might be a good chance to practise her English. She asked him how he came to be there. And in an accent just like Miss Adelia's, he told her all about his life in Changi with his British ex-Navy uncle. Lili told Lizard that she wanted him to teach her to talk like he did, and she outlined her plan for him to live in one of the cubicles above her father's tailor shop. She'd also told him about the mission school that took a few boys for free each year. And so Lizard became her friend and made his home in Chinatown.

Lili frowned. Distracted again! By Lizard. She mentally pushed him aside and locked up the equipment room.

CHAPTER FIVE

Strange Behaviour at Fatty Dim Sum's Coffee Shop

Lizard slouched dejectedly as he walked along South Bridge Road on his way home from school. He hadn't seen Lili since she had stormed inside after cleaning his split lip last night. He had looked for her outside the gates of her school to apologise, although he still didn't know what he'd done wrong.

The teak box was back in his satchel and he didn't know what to do with it. It seemed to be getting heavier. Lizard was in two minds: half of him was thrilled with agitated curiosity, sure that it was connected to Uncle Archie; but the other half wished he had never stolen the box, reasoning that it was trouble, and that there was no actual evidence it had anything to do with his uncle.

Chinatown people were superstitious to the

marrow—to Lizard the box couldn't have been more unlucky if it were wrapped in white sackcloth with the number four written all over it and had two upright chopsticks poking out the top. Lizard thought about flinging it over the side of the bridge, but the idea of maybe bringing on even worse luck stopped him. Although what else could possibly go wrong?

'*Wei!* Boy!'

Lizard heard footsteps hurrying up behind him. 'Oh, no, no, no!' Lizard moaned out loud. He turned, fists clenched.

'Hey, don't be so anxious, my friend!' said Brylcreem, speaking in English, grinning widely and holding his palms up.

Buck Tooth mooched along beside him with his hands in his pockets. '*Wah*, you look so smart in your white school clothes. Even got white, white shoes!' Brylcreem said.

Lizard raised his eyebrows. He flinched as Brylcreem flung an arm around his shoulders.

'Sorry about yesterday. Your name Lizard, right?

My girlfriend, Ting Ha, she tell me you are friend of her cousin, Lili. Why you not say?' said Brylcreem expansively.

'What?' Lizard was confused by this turn of events. Ting Ha was Lili's cousin whose pocket he had tried to pick two years ago.

Brylcreem gave a little laugh. His right arm was still heavy around Lizard's shoulder. 'My girlfriend, she tell me off for fighting with you,' he said.

'She always telling somebody off,' muttered Buck Tooth.

Brylcreem turned on him and gave him a shove. 'Shut up, you! What you say about my girlfriend, hah? Hah?'

'Nothing, nothing,' said Buck Tooth, sulking.

Brylcreem peered at Lizard's swollen lip. '*Wah*, sorry, ah? No need to tell Ting Ha I did that, all right?'

Lizard nodded. He noticed that Brylcreem's eye was only a little bruised.

'Listen, you know Ting Ha's uncle is Inspector at the Tanjong Pagar Police Station?' said Brylcreem.

'Ting Ha want me to become a policeman. Do something new, she say. What you think?'

'Uh—good idea. Yes, a really good idea,' said Lizard, who didn't know Ting Ha's uncle and didn't care what Brylcreem's life ambitions were.

'You think so? Good, good. Because Ting Ha say you can help me. With studying, you know? Have to pass a pro-fish-and-see exam to be a policeman.'

'A what? Oh, a *proficiency* exam,' said Lizard.

'Yeah, that's what I say. Anyway, Ting Ha say you so good at studying and a helpful guy. You half-English, so can help me, right?'

'Uh—sure, all right,' Lizard said, in the spirit of self-preservation.

'*Wah*, you so good, man. All right, maybe start tomorrow, or next day?' Brylcreem finally removed his arm from Lizard's shoulders and turned to go.

'Wait a minute,' said Lizard. 'What's your name?'

'Oh, yeah. Forget to tell you, sorry. They call me Brylcreem,' he said, preening his quiff. 'And,' he gestured at his friend. 'He's Buck Tooth.'

There was a pause.

'Really?' asked Lizard.

'Yeah, why?'

'No reason,' said Lizard, turning into Tanjong Pagar Road. He headed towards Sum's Coffee Shop, where he often went after school.

It was only when he stepped inside that he realised that this was the last place he had seen Boss Man Beng alive and well. A wave of sadness and fear hit him, but he didn't have time to dwell on it. The owner of the coffee shop, Fatty Dim Sum, was acting strangely.

Fatty was wiping down a marble-topped table when Lizard entered. That wasn't strange; it was the look of goggle-eyed consternation on Fatty's face when he saw Lizard that was strange.

The greeting Lizard was about to utter died on his lips.

Fatty's eyeballs started jerking repeatedly to his left.

'What?' asked Lizard, staring at Fatty's jerking eyeballs. He went to sit on a stool. Fatty leaned over and started to wipe it. Lizard went to sit on another, but Fatty got there first with his cloth.

'Want a drink, ah, boy?' asked Fatty loudly in Cantonese. His eyeballs had stopped jerking, but now his eyebrows were waggling up and down.

'Ye-es,' Lizard said hesitantly.

'Come to the counter then, boy,' said Fatty, standing straight. To Lizard's relief, Fatty's face stopped twitching.

There was a long horizontal mirror behind the counter. It was spotted with age and humidity. Fatty turned his back to pop the cap off a bottle of raspberry drink, but Lizard could see Fatty's face in the mirror.

He saw Fatty's eyes start jerking again, this time to his right, and Lizard half turned to look in that direction. He stopped at Fatty's glare of horror. Instead, he looked in the mirror and saw the reflection of a man with a shaved head sitting in the corner by the door. Even sitting down he looked big and tall. He held up a newspaper, but his cold, dark eyes were looking over the top of it. At Lizard.

Lizard felt a chill in his neck. Nothing about

the man was friendly. Lizard looked at Fatty in the mirror again, and saw him fold a white cotton cloth into a rectangle, then spill raspberry drink on the counter. He dipped his finger surreptitiously into the liquid and dotted the finger on to the rectangle. Lizard stared at the red circle on the white rectangle. It looked just like the Japanese flag.

Fatty glanced at Lizard, satisfied that he finally understood, and blew his nose noisily into the white cloth. He turned from the mirror and handed the bottle of drink to Lizard.

Fatty always had the radio playing in the background and often sang along in a high reedy voice if a Hokkien song was on. As Lizard paid for his drink, Fatty started singing a familiar chorus but he changed the words to 'Jackfruit tree, see you, my dear, at the jackfruit tree'. The previous hundred times Lizard had heard Fatty sing that song, the tree had been a magnolia tree.

Lizard left with his raspberry drink. He tried to look relaxed even though he could feel the Japanese man's eyes burning into him as he walked out the door. He stepped into the five-foot way and sighed with relief—prematurely, as it turned out. A tea vendor cycled past and Lizard saw, reflected in the huge metallic drum of tea on the back of the bicycle, that the tall Japanese man was coming up behind him.

Just as the man's meaty hand, large and menacing in the reflection, reached out for Lizard's shoulder, Lizard jumped across the monsoon drain in front of the five-foot way and collided with the tea seller's drum. The bicycle and its rider went over with a clattering crash, and hot fragrant tea swished all over the road. Lizard spun his arms around as if trying to keep his balance. Raspberry drink spiralled into the air, some splattering the face of the Japanese man who had followed him onto the road. The half-empty bottle glanced off the man's head, then smashed in the monsoon drain.

'*Wah*, sorry, ah!' Lizard said, as he made himself fall, slamming into the chest of the man. He planted an elbow hard into the man's abdomen, and they both landed on the road at the drain's edge. A second bicycle swerved to avoid them and the man riding it, along with his wife and a basketful of eggs, fell onto the steaming, tea-washed road.

Lizard leapt up and looked with horrified fascination at the mess he had made. Four people were sprawled in the road weltering in tea and smashed eggs. Traffic came to a halt and people stopped to watch, comment and add to the uproar. Fatty Dim Sum's startled face goggled through the coffee shop window in between the golden roast ducks hung up to air, but Fatty wisely stayed inside. The Japanese man sat up, blinked and wiped his eyes. Then those eyes started scanning the scene, no doubt looking for Lizard.

Lizard turned and hustled through the crowd. After passing several shops he ducked behind a pillar and squatted next to a little girl who was playing behind a woman selling vegetables in the five-foot way.

The little girl looked at him. 'What are we playing?' she asked in Cantonese.

'Hide and seek,' Lizard said. He stuck his head out cautiously to see if the Japanese man was still there. Yes, there he was, a head taller than everyone else. He had raspberry stains down his shirt and a hostile look on his face. Lizard gulped and uttered a few Cantonese swear words.

The little girl repeated them. 'What does that mean?' she asked.

'No, no, don't say that. Your mother won't like it.' Lizard leaned back against the pillar. 'I have to hide now. Don't give me away, all right?'

She nodded, giggling. She peeked around the pillar. 'Is it that tall ugly man who's looking for you?' she asked.

Lizard nodded, put a finger to his lips and then sneaked behind a large basket of cabbages. He looked into the monsoon drain, and then at his white, white school shoes. With a sigh, he took them off, tied the laces together and slung the shoes around his neck. He stepped into the drain. Even though he was used to running barefoot every day, he grimaced as he sank ankle deep into the stinking sludge.

He looked under the concrete slab that formed a bridge across the drain. The space under it was just big enough for him to squeeze into. Trying not to get his clothes or his satchel in the sludge, he manoeuvred himself in. Lucky for him it hadn't rained since the night before and the water level was low. Sweat trickled down his face as he settled in the smelly, stifling, cramped place. He really hoped he wouldn't have to wait there all afternoon.

Lizard willed the Japanese man not to notice the small Chinese girl squatting against the pillar giggling behind her hands at apparently nothing and just keep on stomping angrily down the road.

A few minutes later, an upside-down head with two bunches of hair appeared over the side of the slab.

'*Wei*, the ugly guy's gone. You win,' the little girl said. She wrinkled her nose. 'You stink to death, but you win.'

'Are you sure he's gone?' Lizard asked.

'He went past the peanut seller, and then I couldn't see him anymore,' she said.

Lizard crawled out from under the concrete slab, glanced warily round and climbed out of the drain.

'Thanks,' he said to the girl, and he hurried down the road, ignoring the stares that people gave him as he passed by emitting the fragrance eau de drain.

Ten minutes later, Lizard was in the back lane behind the Tanjong Pagar wet market at the jackfruit tree, a popular meeting spot where the local children gathered to play marbles. He hoped it was the right jackfruit tree. He had rinsed himself off with a standpipe by the street, but he was still quite smelly. He was relieved when Fatty Dim Sum hurried past the fruit sellers and squatted down next to him. Fatty sniffed, then moved away a little.

'Don't look at me,' hissed Fatty, lighting up a cigarette. 'You're a good boy, Lizard. Yes, I know you steal, but you don't steal from me. I don't want you to die like Ah Beng.'

'Me neither,' said Lizard, perched on the low brick wall of the wet market. He crouched down and started to put his shoes back on slowly, not looking at Fatty.

'Lucky you got away,' said Fatty. 'Maybe the Japanese know you work with Ah Beng. I don't say anything. But they have spies everywhere. That Japanese guy, Katsu, he's a gunjin spy I think—'

'What's gunjin?' asked Lizard.

'Gunjin is Japanese army or navy man. He hang round my shop, ask questions. He ask about Ah Beng. Where he live, what he do, who he talk to. He even give me money to talk.'

'You didn't take his money?' said Lizard, impressed. Chinatown businessmen would generally agree to sell you their last grandmother if you paid cash.

'Of course I take it!' said Fatty, affronted. 'Otherwise he suspicious. I give it to Ah Ling for the Anti-Japan War in China Fund.' He spat happily into the open drain. 'I tell him small stuff. Not important. But that Ah Beng, he got a big mouth. Got himself killed. The gunjin think he stole something important from them. Something secret. Something'—here his voice dropped even lower—'that could make them lose the war.'

'The war in China?' asked Lizard, putting a hand on his satchel.

'Must be,' said Fatty. 'Unless they starting some other war.' He sucked on his cigarette and stood up. 'You be careful. That's all I want to say. Keep quiet. Stay out of trouble.'

He stared at something in the wet market for a long time. Lizard followed his gaze and found himself looking at a cage stuffed full with live chickens, their heads sticking out through the wires. They weren't clucking; they just waited.

'I'm scared of the gunjin. In China, they are very cruel,' Fatty Dim Sum said. 'That's why we Chinese don't want to use Japanese stuff now, or go to Japanese shops. We blame the shopkeepers, even though it's the gunjin who do the killing.'

Lizard thought about the Japanese people that he knew. Mostly they were in Middle Road near Raffles Hotel and ran shops selling things like textiles and silk goods. The Japanese doctors and dentists had their offices there too. There was also Mr Nakajima who had the photographic studio round the back of Raffles Hotel. None of them had ever shown any inclination to hurt him. Maybe being only half

Chinese was good for something after all.

'The Japanese shopkeepers in Middle Road aren't cruel,' Lizard said. 'It's not fair to blame them.'

'It's the soldiers that kill. The gunjin don't tell the ordinary Japanese people what they do. But some of them are spies, Lizard. That's the trouble, eh. We don't know who is normal Japanese person and who is a gunjin spy,' said Fatty Dim Sum. 'Don't come to my shop now. Katsu will be watching.' He smiled sadly at Lizard. 'The world is changing, Lizard. I feel it. The world is changing.'

Lizard headed for home, cutting through the wet market, past sellers weighing wriggling crabs, avoiding the buckets of water everywhere and resisting the temptation to steal a ripe mango from a laden fruit stall. As he left the market, he saw a shaved head bobbing above the crowd. Katsu! Was he still looking for Lizard?

Without a second thought, Lizard followed him. He was careful to stay well behind and in the thick of the crowd. This might be his chance to find out more about the strange book in the box. Lizard followed the bobbing shaved head of the unpretty Katsu all the way up South Bridge Road and over the Elgin Bridge. Katsu looked behind a few times, but Lizard found it easy to avoid being seen in the colourful commotion of the road.

Katsu continued on to North Bridge Road and then turned left into Middle Road. Lizard hurried to catch up. As he rounded the corner, he noticed it was less busy here. He ducked behind a concrete post and cautiously looked out. Street sweeper, yes. Ladies in kimonos, yes. Hawkers and amahs, yes. Tall, ugly gunjin spy, no. He had lost him somewhere in Middle Road.

CHAPTER SIX

The Lazy Gardener

Lili put down the watering can and adjusted the wide-brimmed straw hat she was wearing. She had found both lying by the garden shed at the back of Raffles Hotel. Few people were around as she moved into the Palm Court garden. Perhaps everyone was having an afternoon nap.

Here was suite seventy, where the Whitford Joneses were guests. Lili stepped behind a bush that screened her from the front door, making sure the turbaned soldier standing guard hadn't seen her. She peeked through the leaves of the bush as Commander Baxter of the Royal Navy came into the passageway. He looked just like his photo in the mission file, only a lot more worried.

'I don't expect much action tonight, Singh. The

horse has bolted, I'm afraid. At least Mrs Whitford Jones will feel better with a guard at the door,' Commander Baxter said, lighting a cigarette.

'Yessir,' the guard said.

Lili crouched down and pulled out some scruffy plants which she hoped were weeds.

A man came out. Lili recognised him as Sebastian Whitford Jones. She was curious to see if he looked like the kind of man who would betray his country for money. All she could tell was that he looked genuinely distressed as he accepted the cigarette that Commander Baxter offered him. She would have to wait and see. The two men strolled out into the courtyard garden.

'I had no idea it was so important, Commander. None,' Sebastian Whitford Jones burst out.

'I blame myself, Sebastian. I was sure that the low-key approach would keep the Japanese Navy from knowing it was here,' Commander Baxter said.

'Are you sure it was the Japanese who took it, then?' said Mr Whitford Jones.

The commander gave a bitter bark of laughter.

'Can't really be sure of anything. It might have been the Nazis, except they're so busy with the war in Europe...'

'Do you think Japan will join the war?' said Mr Whitford Jones.

'I think it's likely,' said the commander.

'Terrible business in Shanghai, eh? Even women and children,' said Mr Whitford Jones. 'Why on Earth were the soldiers so ruthless?'

Behind the bush, Lili shuddered, but she had a job to do, and she couldn't afford to let her feelings get in the way.

'It all comes from the top. The new Japanese military command uses brutality to control things, even within their own troops,' said Commander Baxter.

Lili took out her miniature camera. She angled it through the leaves and took a few shots of the two men. Judging by the conversation, the commander didn't seem to suspect Mr Whitford Jones of being a traitor.

'About this box. I wasn't told what was in it,' said

Mr Whitford Jones. 'Do you know?'

'No, it's top secret,' Commander Baxter admitted.

Lili was startled. She knew what was in the box; she knew this secret and the navy commander didn't. For the first time, she felt the heavy responsibility of belonging to a covert intelligence organisation.

'It's really that important, is it?' said Mr Whitford Jones.

'So the captain says.' Lili could see the commander's pained hunch even through the leaves. 'Had rather an unpleasant interview with him this morning. If you hear a clunk from across town, it will be my head dropping onto the Persian carpet in his office.'

'*We're* not actually at war with the Japanese, are we?' asked Mr Whitford Jones. 'Can't we just let the Asiatics fight it out among themselves?'

Commander Baxter took a deep, controlling breath in through his nostrils.

Lili sympathised. Mr Whitford Jones seemed too dull to be able to organise the sale of sensitive secrets to a foreign power like Japan.

'Don't underestimate the Japanese Empire, Sebastian,' said Commander Baxter. 'They need land. They need oil and rubber and tin and so forth. The entire Indochina area is valuable, including Malaya, and what's at the end of the Malayan Peninsula? Singapore. Jewel of the East and a slap in the face for the British if the Japanese take her.'

'Japan can't just take over a country because it feels like it,' said Mr Whitford Jones.

'Why not? We did.' Commander Baxter stubbed out his cigarette vigorously in the ashtray on a nearby table. 'We've been taking over countries for centuries. That's what an empire *is*, Sebastian.'

'Well, if you say so,' Mr Whitford Jones said doubtfully. 'Just doesn't seem right.'

'Because we don't want to share. The Japanese want Asia for their empire and will fight with European powers to get it. It's a fight we must win. So, no, we can't just let the Asiatics fight it out themselves.'

'So we need the box, then?' Mr Whitford Jones said.

'Absolutely. We've been questioning the staff all

day. Had to get a Hainanese interpreter. Not all the staff speak English.' Commander Baxter straightened his uniform. 'Right. I'd best be getting back. Singh will be on guard all night.'

He headed off, towards the main building, and Sebastian Whitford Jones went back inside.

Lili didn't think Mr Whitford Jones sounded like a man who had sold out the British. However, it was possible that he was only pretending to be dull, and that he was double crossing Commander Baxter. She needed to keep watching Mr Whitford Jones.

The shadows had lengthened right across the garden and the birds were making a big racket as they jostled for the best positions in the trees. It would be dark soon, and the gardeners didn't work at night, so Lili couldn't stay in the Palm Court disguised as one. She waited until the Sikh guard was called inside, and then she abandoned the hat and watering can behind the bush and scrambled up the pillars and balustrades of the building and onto the roof. If Sebastian Whitford Jones was going to meet anyone secretly, the roof would be a great spot to observe the rendezvous. She lay down on the warm roof tiles and peered over the edge. She could see the bush near suite seventy. There was someone in the shadows where she had been hiding. She gulped at her close escape.

Lizard waited until after sunset before slipping in to the Palm Court, carrying the teak box in his satchel. As he ducked behind a bush near the door of suite seventy, he stubbed his toe on a heavy watering can. He thought unkind thoughts about lazy gardeners who left watering cans lying around.

The door of suite seventy opened. Lizard's eyes bulged with alarm as a big, bearded Sikh soldier came out, closed the door and planted himself in front of it as if he would be there all night. Lizard cursed his bad luck. How would he get to see Georgina and ask her about the teak box now? He needed to find another way to sneak in to suite seventy.

Time to visit his friend Roshan.

Since the Palm Court was a guest-only area, Lizard needed a disguise. He reached out and picked up the watering can and a hat lying next to it, taking back his previous harsh thoughts about the lazy gardener. He stepped out from behind the bush and kept close to the hedges along the walkway, avoiding the moonlight and hoping he wouldn't be noticed even though he had his gardener's disguise.

On the rooftop, Lili realised that her position was fine for watching the garden, but that she couldn't see the covered walkway in front of the suite. The lamps around the Palm Court were now lit. For a moment, a figure below reminded her of Lizard, but of course it couldn't be him. It must be a real gardener, tidying away the hat and watering can. She gave herself an angry shake and vowed not to let stray thoughts of Lizard distract her again.

Lizard went round the back of the Bras Basah wing of the hotel on his way to the staff area. He surreptitiously dropped the hat and the watering can by the wall. As he was passing the Raffles Photographic Studio, Mr

Nakajima popped out. '*Konbanwa*, Lizard-san,' he said, and bowed.

'*Konbanwa*, Nakajima-san,' Lizard said, returning the bow.

Then, Mr Nakajima said in a hushed voice, 'You hear, Lizard-san? Stealing happening here! Yes!' He bobbed his head. 'At Raffles Hotel! How can be? So impolite!'

Lizard didn't want to waste time, but the man looked so horrified and dejected that he stopped. 'Oh, yes, I did hear something.' He groaned inwardly as his ears heard what his mouth had just said. He should have said no, he hadn't heard.

'You heard? What did you hear? Did your friend Roshan say something?' Mr Nakajima darted forward. Lizard had enjoyed cups of *genmaicha*— roasted rice green tea—with Mr Nakajima. The man had a thirst for gossip and company. Lizard thought he must be lonely, stuck in the darkroom of his studio for hours on end, developing film into photographs.

'No, I haven't seen Roshan yet. I'm just going there now,' Lizard said.

'Come in and have some *genmaicha*. I remember how you like it.' He gave a little bow of invitation and extended a hand towards his studio. 'This terrible thing is bad for business. I have some seaweed snacks fresh in too.'

'Well, maybe for a short time,' said Lizard, suddenly hungry for green tea and seaweed snacks.

'What have you got there?' Mr Nakajima gestured at Lizard's bag.

'Oh,' Lizard said, putting his hand on it. 'Nothing. Just some school books.'

Mr Nakajima nodded, as he ushered Lizard into the studio. 'You not seen Roshan yet? Who tell you about the stealing then?'

'No one. I don't know anything about the stealing, I just saw a lot of soldiers and police in the driveway,' Lizard lied. 'What was stolen?'

'They will not say, but I think it must have been something very valuable,' said Mr Nakajima, pursing his lips.

He waved at the small wooden table he kept at the left side of the studio and hurried off through a side door on the right to prepare the tea. Lizard followed him to the doorway. He glimpsed a windowless room with a sink and jars of chemicals on a shelf. This was the darkroom where Mr Nakajima developed his photographs.

'Need any help?' Lizard asked.

'No!' said Mr Nakajima, whirling round and hurrying back to Lizard. He made flapping motions at Lizard and half-closed the door. 'You sit! Sit!'

Lizard backed out into the large studio, where Mr Nakajima photographed people. He also took his camera gear to the Raffles Tea Dances to take pictures of the glamorous couples there.

On the left, past the table, were pretty screens that he used as backdrops, as well as various props neatly organised along the wall. A large, elegant crackle-glazed turquoise vase sat on a shelf next to the screens. Lizard knew it was Mr Nakajima's favourite possession. It was given to him by his mother and he had brought it with him from his home island of Awaji in Japan.

Lizard looked at the photographs displayed

on the wall next to the darkroom door. They were mostly of British army officers and their well-groomed wives in their best frocks, although there were also photographs of Singapore Harbour, some huge boats in a dock, various cityscapes and a few beaches. With a bittersweet jolt, Lizard recognised one as Changi beach, near his old home.

He leaned in, looking at the coconut palms by the beach. Several people stood under the trees. Might one of them be Uncle Archie? They were too far away to make out clearly. As he peered at the photograph, Mr Nakajima returned, shutting the darkroom door firmly behind him.

'Come, Lizard-san! Sit down, have some tea.'

'I thought you only took photographs of people.' Lizard's eyes lingered on the Changi beach photograph as he sat down at the table and put his bag on the floor.

'People, buildings, beaches, ships, planes; Nakajima takes photographs of all Singapore. I take photographs for the newspaper, you know. Even for the British Navy. Photographs of the British

Naval Base. Very beautiful.' Chuckling to himself, he put down the plate of snacks and poured out the tea, settling himself on a chair next to Lizard. The fragrant smell of roasted rice tea wafted into Lizard's nostrils.

Just as Lizard was about to pick up his cup, he was startled to hear sweet piping chirps. 'What's that?' he said, looking at the far corner of the studio from where the sound came.

'Ah!' said Mr Nakajima with a smile. 'Marvellous! That is the first time my new pet has sung its beautiful song.'

Lizard saw a paper-covered screen on a table. There must be a bird in a cage behind the screen.

'My little *uguisu*. In Japan, people believe spring has arrived when we hear the song of the *uguisu* bird.' He took a sip of his tea. 'You bring me luck, young Lizard. I have had it a month and this is the first time it sings.'

'Why is it behind the screen?'

'It encourages them to sing if you block out some of the light. Excuse me, Lizard-san, I must check it has enough water.' He stepped to the table in the corner and moved the screen aside. He murmured softly in Japanese to the bird, while pouring water for it. Lizard craned his head and caught a glimpse of a beak through the bamboo bars of the cage. Mr Nakajima reached in and stroked the bird with a finger.

Lizard thought it must be hot and boring behind that screen. He wouldn't feel like singing if he was stuck in that corner. 'Can I see it?' he asked.

'Oh, it is nothing special to look at. Only its song is beautiful. Anyway, terrible thing, this stealing, isn't it?' Mr Nakajima sat back down again. 'What did you see outside?'

'Just…some soldiers walking around.' Lizard helped himself to some seaweed snacks.

Mr Nakajima raised his eyebrows and looked eagerly at Lizard, nodding.

'And Mr Arathoon, looking not very happy,' said Lizard, munching. Mr Arathoon was the manager of the hotel.

Mr Nakajima nodded again at Lizard, not saying anything.

'And a Sikh guard outside the door.'

'Oh? You could see all that from the back of the hotel?' Mr Nakajima's tone was mild, but his eyes were shrewd.

Lizard gulped. 'It wasn't dark yet,' he stammered. 'And I saw a Sikh soldier walking with another soldier—you know how it's often the Sikhs who are guards and that—so I just guessed that's what he would be doing.' He jumped up. 'I have to go now. Thank you so much for the tea, Mr Nakajima.' Lizard snatched up his satchel, ducked a quick bow and ran out the door.

'Goodbye, Lizard-san,' said Mr Nakajima to Lizard's departing back. He stood up and walked to the door. He remained there, staring after Lizard as he ran into the night.

Lizard mentally kicked himself as he ran round the back way to the staff area. Stupid! Why did he stop to speak to the man? Never mind, he told himself. Mr Nakajima was harmless, just very chatty.

As Lizard opened the door into the staffroom he felt his shoulders relax. This was where the staff came during their breaks or before their shifts started. Here he didn't need to be on guard. He found Roshan, who was sprawled on a couch, making rich, bubbling snores.

Lizard grinned as he looked down at his sleeping friend. He thought about waking him with water or some other similarly amusing method but he didn't have the time for that.

'Hey, Roshan, wake up.' Lizard shook Roshan's shoulder, firmly enough to wake him but not hard enough to put him into a bad mood.

'What? Hey?' said Roshan sitting bolt upright. 'Am I late?'

'No, I don't think so,' said Lizard.

'Oh, Lizard, it's just you.' Roshan rubbed his eyes and yawned. 'What you doing here?'

'I need to talk to you. It's important,' said Lizard.

'Lucky for you I'm doing room-boy duty tonight or I'd be in the dining room now,' said Roshan, stretching.

'What? The maitre'd fire you, ah? Make too many mistakes, ah?' said Lizard with a grin.

'No, they arrested one of the Palm Court room boys so I have to fill in. Ah Hong—you know Ah Hong? Been here fifteen years already, and now they suddenly accuse him of stealing. Big hullabaloo here last night, you know.' Roshan finally looked wide awake. 'I'm supposed to be in suite seventy now except the guests wanted a few hours alone, no hotel staff.'

'What happened?' asked Lizard, his heart thudding heavily as he stared at his friend.

'The big shot English boss, New East India Company guy, said somebody stole something from his suite. Said maybe Ah Hong did it.' Roshan shook his head. 'Not possible. That fellow never even took used soap home! He was crying when the police came—police *and* soldiers. So many British officers. You never seen anything like it. Police say they in charge, soldiers say they in charge. Man, they wouldn't even say what was stolen. I think must be all the crown jewels.'

'Did they say anything about me?' said Lizard, worried that Georgina Whitford Jones might have told them about his visit last night.

'You? No, why would they?' said Roshan.

'Never mind. Then what happened?' Lizard said.

'Then I think the soldiers won. Took Ah Hong away. They tell Mr Arathoon he must get the whole staff ready to be questioned. So we were all questioned the whole day,' said Roshan. He noticed Lizard staring at him in terror. '*Wah*, what happened to your mouth? Fight again, ah? And why you look at me so like that?' He goggled his eyes at Lizard in demonstration.

Lizard took a deep breath. He had to pull himself together or he was sunk. 'Roshan. We been friends a long time, right?'

'Yeah, man, I guess.'

'I saved your life the first time we met, right?'

'Well, I don't know. I don't think that old aunty would really have killed me for tripping over her banana fritters basket.' Roshan guffawed. 'And I would have climbed the drainpipe all right even if you hadn't pulled me up.'

'I need your help, Roshan. I know Ah Hong

didn't steal the thing.' Lizard looked around the room. It was otherwise empty as everyone else was on duty. He dropped his voice to a whisper. 'Because I did.'

'What? Ha ha!' Roshan laughed uneasily. 'I thought you said you stole the...whatever the thing is.'

'I did! And I wish I'd never seen it!' Lizard dropped his face into his cupped hands.

'Why you take it, then? You crazy?' said Roshan, waving his hands at his friend.

'I didn't know it would cause so much trouble!' said Lizard. 'I thought it was just another job Boss Man Beng wanted me to do. He's dead, you know— they killed him! With a big knife!'

'What? Who killed him? For the—what did you steal?' Roshan's face was ablaze with shock and fear and curiosity.

'I don't know who killed him. And the thing is—' Lizard stopped short. He didn't want to tell Roshan that he felt that the thing had something to do with his Uncle Archie and that he needed to know if the box was connected with his uncle's disappearance.

Roshan's gaze dropped to Lizard's satchel. He raised his eyebrows at Lizard. Lizard nodded grimly.

'Trust me, it's better if you don't know. It's bad luck, that's what it is. Really bad luck. Ask Boss Man Beng—oh, wait, you can't, because he's *dead*.'

'Why you don't throw it away, then?' Roshan made no move towards the box, though his horrified eyes were riveted to it.

'They won't stop looking until they find it. They'll search until they find me. And if I don't have it, then they'll think I've hidden it.' He looked at Roshan. 'You've got to help me put it back or I'll be dead too! And if I die I'll come back every night and haunt you!' He jabbed his finger into Roshan's chest.

Roshan furrowed his brow.

'Every single night. *Whooo*.' Lizard leaned forward and draped his hands in the air. 'Like that.'

'If I help you and you die anyway, will you still haunt me?' asked Roshan.

'No, because then it's my own stupid fault.'

'All right, I'll help you.' Roshan rummaged

around in his pocket. 'Here, I'll give you something to help with your bad luck.' He dropped a handful of bright red, roundish seeds into Lizard's hand. They were shiny and hard and about the size of small blueberries.

'Saga seeds?' Lizard said, puzzled.

'Not just ordinary saga seeds—lucky red seeds. My brother got them from Travancore, when he went to India last time to see the great man Gandhi speak. He gave me a big jar of them. He says the seeds are especially lucky when they are from Travancore. I always carry some with me, and I've been promoted twice this year already.'

Lizard shrugged and pocketed the seeds. He needed all the luck he could get.

'Now what you need me to do?' Roshan asked.

'I need you to get me into suite seventy,' said Lizard.

An hour later, Lizard was hiding in the bottom of the dinner trolley as Roshan pushed it into the Palm Court wing of the Raffles Hotel. The trolley was covered with a large, white table cloth. As Roshan pushed it into suite seventy, he positioned it between the Indian maid who answered the door and the bedroom.

'Good evening, madam, here is the dinner,' Roshan said cheerfully.

Lizard scurried into the bedroom. He crouched beside the bed and waited until he heard the maid showing Roshan out. Then he slipped into the wardrobe and closed the door. Time for more waiting.

CHAPTER SEVEN

The Bag, the Box and the Boy

The clothes in the wardrobe were mostly dresses, small dresses. Lizard folded himself into the furthest corner and sat with the satchel in his lap. Outside, people came and went. Once, heart-stoppingly, the wardrobe door opened and the maid took out a dress. Luckily, she hadn't wanted shoes or she might have found herself bending to reach them and looking into Lizard's terrified eyes.

Eventually, the household noises settled down, and Lizard heard Georgina come into the room and get into bed.

'Here is your night-time milk, Missy Georgina,' said her maid. There was a soft clink as she put the glass down on the bedside table. 'You sure you be all right by yourself? You want I sleep in here with you?'

'Don't fuss so, Ruksana. You're like a fussy hen, always clucking about,' Georgina said. 'I don't want you here tonight. I'm very tired so I don't want you to disturb me at all. You understand? If you come in and wake me up, I shall be very cross and I'll tell Father.'

Then Lizard knew that Georgina hadn't forgotten that she had told him—no, blackmailed him—into coming back tonight. Surely she must have worked out that he had taken the thing that everyone was looking for. He didn't understand how she could have held back from telling her parents, the army or the police.

'Yes, Missy Georgina.' Ruksana sounded put out. 'No need to be grumpish. All right, I see you in the morning.' And she muttered under her breath, 'More and more like the memsahib every day...'

'Close the door,' Georgina called.

Lizard heard the door shut, very firmly.

He waited until all was quiet. Georgina's light was still on. He knocked softly on the wardrobe door.

Georgina rustled, then stopped. 'Hello?' she called in a quiet voice.

He knocked again, not wanting to startle her. The bed creaked, and quiet footsteps padded to the wardrobe.

Georgina pulled open the door. 'Is that you, boy?'

Lizard blinked. 'Yes, here.'

'It was you, wasn't it?' she said, crouching down. A lock of clean, red hair fell forward and brushed Lizard's nose. 'You took it, didn't you, Dinesh? I mean...what's your name, again?'

'Dinesh,' said Lizard. 'I mean, Lizard.'

'Oh, I shall just call you Dinesh. It's much easier to remember.'

He looked into her eyes, which were wide open and sparkling with excitement. They were just as blue as he remembered.

'The commotion there's been around here! I haven't seen so much fuss since a cobra was found in the dining room. Anyway, you must show me this thing. No one will tell me what it is,' said Georgina.

Lizard started to crawl out, glad for the chance to stretch his cramped legs.

'No, stay in the wardrobe. Just in case Ruksana decides to check on me even though I forbade her to. Servants can be contrary like that.'

Lizard sat back reluctantly.

'I didn't tell them about you breaking in last night.' She sounded pleased with herself. 'I knew if I did, you would be arrested and I wouldn't ever find out what this so very mysterious thing is.'

'Oh, thank you,' said Lizard. His heart gave an extra thump at the mention of being arrested.

'Wait, I'd better check that Ruksana's not still here,' said Georgina, opening the door and glancing around the room. 'Good, she's not. Now show me the thing.'

'Do you know anything about it?' Lizard asked. 'Perhaps where your father got it from?' Lizard's desperation to find out anything about the book gave him the courage to ask.

'No, of course I don't. That's why I want you to show it to me.'

'I thought you might have heard your father talking about it?'

'I've no idea who he got it from. Probably from someone at the company.'

'Which company?' asked Lizard.

'*The* company—surely even you've heard of it. The New British East India Company. But I don't really know,' said Georgina. She gestured impatiently at Lizard sitting in the bottom of her wardrobe. 'Given the circumstances, it's not as if I can just ask him, is it? Come along, hand it over.'

Lizard was disappointed that Georgina had no information about the box. He held his satchel out.

Georgina snatched it. She took out the teak box and let the satchel fall to the floor. 'At last,' she said, holding the box.

Meanwhile Lili, who was still on the roof, was getting worried. She couldn't hear or see what was happening inside, and nobody had come out into the garden since Mr Whitford Jones and Commander Baxter went back inside. Her previous position behind the bush had been much better for observation. Surely it would be safe there now that it was fully dark. She sneaked to the corner of the building, out of sight of the Sikh soldier, and climbed down.

She scampered to the bushes. The watering can and hat were no longer there; she was impressed by the efficiency of the gardeners.

As she moved behind the bush, her attention was caught by a dim light. She carefully manoeuvred herself so that she could see into the bedroom and took out the miniature spyglass.

Georgina Whitford Jones was sitting in front of the open wardrobe, talking as if to someone in the wardrobe. Who could it be? The open wardrobe door obscured her view.

Then two hands emerged, holding out a familiar-looking satchel to Georgina, who took a box out and dropped the satchel on the floor. Was that the teak box—the object of Lili's extremely important mission? Lili moved as close to the action as she could, but the white balustrade of the walkway in front of the suite prevented her from getting right up to the window.

Through the spyglass, she could see Georgina's lips moving. It was frustrating that she couldn't hear what she was saying. Lili wished she knew who was in the wardrobe.

A moment later, her wish was granted. She focused the spyglass on the satchel. No wonder that discarded bag looked familiar: she'd made it for Lizard herself, from her father's tailoring offcuts.

'What!' Lili exclaimed under her breath when she realised that it must be Lizard in the wardrobe. Lili couldn't see him, but she had no doubt it was him. Not just talking to that girl, but showing her the teak box! Her head reeled at this sudden collision of her two worlds, which, until this moment, had been completely separate. How could Lizard be mixed up with her Max Ops mission?

Blue eyes! Red hair! She fumed. Now she knew exactly who Lizard had been talking about yesterday.

Inside the room, Georgina was smiling. 'How exciting!' she exclaimed.

'Not for me,' Lizard said.

'Don't worry,' Georgina said, with a sly glance at him. 'I won't give you away—as long as you do what I say.'

She opened the box, took out the parcel and tore the cord and brown paper off. Then she opened the book. 'What does it say?' she asked Lizard, frowning at the pages.

Lizard shrugged. 'I've no idea. Why don't you ask your father?' There was no way now for Lizard to find out any more about the box, and the flame of hope that it could lead him to Uncle Archie fizzled out. 'I'll be going now,' he said. He was relieved that at least he could get away from the bad-luck box.

'You stay in there. Maybe there's some sort of secret writing on the box or the book that you can only see by moonlight!' Georgina said. 'I read about that in my *Schoolgirls' Own Annual*.'

'I don't think that's likely,' Lizard said.

Lili was furious. The little English madam had Lili's bag, Lili's box and Lili's boy. Time to fix that, she thought. Then she frowned. She was distracted again!

Focus on the mission, she told herself. Her actual mission brief was the surveillance of Mr Whitford Jones, but the ultimate goal for Max Ops was to get the box containing the codebook, and it was right there in front of her. She shoved the spyglass in her pocket to free up her hands. Now, how was she going to do this?

She watched as Georgina leaned her head out the window and looked at the turbaned soldier standing near the front door.

'Good evening, Mr Singh,' said Georgina, with the boldness of undeserved entitlement. 'I'm opening the window wider to let fresh air into the room. The heat is so tiresome.'

'Yes, Miss Georgina,' said the soldier, and he turned to look the other way.

Georgina ducked her head back into the room and held the teak box up, angling it to catch the moonlight.

Lili was so intent on watching Georgina that she did not notice a man appear over the edge of the roofline above her, close to where she had been only a few moments before. The man lowered himself down onto the first-floor balcony and then dropped lightly into the shrubbery below.

Both Lili and the Sikh soldier heard the man landing and turned to look in that direction. A black-clad figure popped up and flung something at the soldier.

The soldier clapped a hand to his neck, stumbled and collapsed.

Before Lili could move, the black-clad man leapt over the white balustrade. He stretched an arm in through the window and grabbed at the box that Georgina was holding.

'No!' gasped Georgina, pushing the man's arm away.

Lili recovered herself. She flicked the dagger out of her sleeve and threw it at the man. It thudded into the wooden window frame inches from the man's masked head. The man flinched back.

Georgina held the box tight, but it flipped open in the ruckus and the book fell out.

The man reached in through the window, this

time with both arms. He seized Georgina, yanked her out and sprinted into the garden with her tucked under his arm and the now-empty box tight in her hands.

Lili shot out of the bush and chased after him. The man threw Georgina over the wall bordering Beach Road then vanished over the top himself.

By the time Lili got to the top of the wall, all she could see was a sleek black automobile speeding down Beach Road. She stared helplessly, furious with herself.

When she got back to suite seventy, she was surprised to find that all was quiet. The guard lay on the ground, motionless. She looked in through the open window. Lizard's startled eyes peered around the wardrobe door.

'Lizard!' Lili hissed. 'Come on! Get out of there!' She glanced at the guard who was stirring and groaning. He reached up and pulled a dart from his neck.

Lizard scuttled out of the wardrobe and grabbed his satchel off the floor. 'Who's that? Lili? Is that you?' he whispered in astonishment. 'What are you doing here?'

'No time for that—we have to go!' she whispered. She saw the book on the floor. 'Hey, what's that?'

'Missy Georgina must have dropped it,' said Lizard. 'Where is she? Is she all right?' He started to climb out of the window.

Lili shoved him back. 'Get that book! I need it!'

'But—'

'Now!' she said, giving his arm a tight slap.

'*Ow!*' he said. 'What was that for?'

'*Tch!*' Lili said in disgust. She pushed him aside and dived in through the window, rolling and snatching up the book as she landed. She looked up just in time to see Georgina's maid standing in the doorway staring at her.

Lili turned, clutching the book, and leapt back through the window, dragging Lizard out with her.

'*Aieeee!*' The maid shrieked, like the five-fifteen arriving at Singapore Railway Station.

'Follow me,' Lili gasped. She shoved the book into the front of her tunic, shinnied up a stone pillar and onto the roof. Lizard was right behind her.

'This way,' she said, as uproar broke out below them.

Lizard followed her over the rooftops until they reached Bras Basah Road, where they dropped lightly down and were swallowed up in the crowd.

'So, what happened, Lili? One minute the missy was there, the next gone,' said Lizard, as they strode past a sugarcane-juice vendor.

'Shhh!' Lili said fiercely. 'We'll talk about it later.'

'And what were you doing there?'

'I said shut up!' Lili hissed in Cantonese.

'Well, that's rude,' Lizard said, offended.

They walked until they reached the Singapore River. Lili waved a rickshaw down. 'Can I at least ask where we are going?' Lizard tried again.

'You'll see,' said Lili. 'Sit back. Hide your face.'

Lizard hadn't ridden in a rickshaw since he was little. He listened with an uncomfortable feeling in his chest to the scrawny man's deep, ragged puffing and his feet slapping the road. He was surprised when the rickshaw turned into Tanjong Pagar Road. He was about to ask Lili if they were going home, but the fierce look she gave him closed his mouth right up. As they passed Mak's Tailor Shop, he turned to look at its closed metal grills. Lili sat with her head down.

A few shop houses further down, the rickshaw pulled over and they got out. Lili paid the man, then glanced briefly around the crowded road and vanished up the stairs next to a provisions shop.

'What are we doing here?' asked Lizard, following right behind her.

'Ting Ha lives here,' Lili said. 'That's her family's shop downstairs.' Ting Ha's family was quite well off by Chinatown standards. The upstairs part, from what Lizard could see from the landing, was tidy and there were no partitioned cubicles. The family altar was on a small wooden table by the wall. Above it hung a photograph of a stern old lady with her hair scraped back. She looked like everybody's grandmother.

'Hey, Ting Ju,' Lili said to a girl who looked about seven years old. 'Go get Ting Ha for me, all right?'

Ting Ju disappeared inside, and a moment later

Ting Ha appeared.

'Hey, Lili, Lizard.' Ting Ha looked surprised but pleased to see them. 'Lizard, did Brylcreem ask you to help him?'

'Oh, yes,' said Lizard, who had forgotten all about it until now.

'Ting Ha, Lizard and I need somewhere quiet,' said Lili.

Ting Ha showed them to the room where she and her two sisters slept. Then she left through the beaded curtain.

Lizard and Lili stared at each other for a moment, neither knowing what to say. Lizard glanced around the room. It had an elevated sleeping platform with room underneath for storage and a window that overlooked the road. Lizard was envious of all the space and especially of the window.

'All right, Lizard. What were you doing there, and how did you get the codebook?' Lili demanded as she sat down on the wooden floor.

'Codebook?' asked Lizard as he sat down too.

'This book!' Lili took it out of her tunic and put

it on the floor.

'Is that what it is? A codebook?' asked Lizard.

'Yes. Luckily it fell out of the box when the man kidnapped the girl, and he didn't see it. I distracted him with—' She shut her mouth with a snap.

'The missy got kidnapped? What happened? One moment she was there, the next she was gone,' said Lizard.

'Didn't you see? A man dragged her out the window and took her away.'

'I was in the wardrobe!' exclaimed Lizard. He couldn't believe it. 'How are we going to get her back?'

'What? Never mind about her!' Lili said. She picked up the book and flipped through the pages. 'We have the book. The girl and the box are not important.'

'I think it's your turn to tell me something. What were you doing at Raffles Hotel?' asked Lizard firmly. He was getting a bit fed up with being pushed around by Lili.

CHAPTER EIGHT

Maximum Operations Enterprise

'All right,' said Lili. She had to think about what she could tell him. 'Um…'

'Don't even think about lying,' said Lizard.

'I haven't said anything yet!'

'You always rub your nose when you lie. That's why I win when we play cards. Right now you're rubbing like you have a mosquito bite, and you haven't even started.' He folded his arms. 'So try again. Why were you there? Were you following me?'

'No!' She was outraged. 'It had nothing to do with you at all!'

'Were you trying to steal the box?'

'No! I was trying to get it back.' As soon as she said this, Lili realised that she shouldn't have. Now Lizard's questions were going to get awkward.

'What?' He looked puzzled. 'How did you even know about it? I only took it yesterday, and you've been at school all day, haven't you?'

'What?' Lili's eyebrows shot up. 'Wait a minute. Are you telling me *you* stole the box?'

Lizard nodded.

Lili figured that Mr Whitford Jones was off the hook then. She would have to tell Miss Adelia as soon as possible. It occurred to her that her report for Maximum Ops would have to include Lizard's role in it. 'Have you any idea what you've done?' she said.

'Well, obviously not, or I wouldn't have done it, a hundred dollars or not!' Lizard gripped his hair in frustration. 'Okay, Lili, I'll tell you. Boss Man Beng promised me one hundred dollars to steal this box yesterday. I think, yes, I need a hundred dollars,' Lizard said. 'Then I can give up the stealing for good. Just make money letter writing. When I went to give it to the Boss, he'd been stabbed, and then he died! Under the clock at the railway station! So I ran. I went back to Raffles tonight because I wanted to put the box back. It is bad luck.'

'You have no idea.' Lili shook her head.

'So tell me.'

'I have to get it for…someone,' said Lili. 'I can't tell you who, so don't ask me, all right?'

'Hmm.' Lizard frowned.

Lili could tell it wasn't all right, but that he was going to see what else she would willingly say before challenging her further.

'Who took Georgina?' Lizard asked.

'I think it was a Japanese spy,' said Lili. 'He wanted the book—he mustn't have noticed the book fell out of the box when he took her.'

Lizard's eyes became big circles.

'I bet it was the spy who chased me! And I bet he killed Boss Man Beng!' he gasped.

'Chased you? What do you mean?' said Lili, startled.

'There was a Japanese spy hanging around in Fatty Dim Sum's coffee shop all day today asking questions about Boss Man Beng. Fatty says his name is Katsu. He chased me but I lost him.' Lizard shuddered. 'Fatty warned me to be careful.'

Lizard and Lili stared at each other.

'I need to take this book and put it somewhere safe,' said Lili.

Quick as a frog's tongue, Lizard's hand darted out and swept the book from beneath Lili's hand.

'What about Georgina?' he said. He sat up straight, holding the book tight, and folded his arms again.

'Forget about her.' Lili scowled. 'Don't you understand? It's more important than her.'

'But she's in real danger,' said Lizard. 'Fatty told me the Japanese soldiers are very cruel. It's my fault they've got her, and I have to get her back.'

Lili stared at Lizard. She banished the thought of dead women and children piled up in the streets of a Chinese city. 'That book is really important. I need to get it to—' She stopped.

'To who?' Lizard's green eyes bored into her. 'Secrets! You always have secrets. You know all about me, but *you* are always hiding stuff. Ever since I've known you, there's been something. Odd injuries, lying about where you've been, sneaking around strange places. What aren't you telling me?'

Lili thought she had always managed to hide her Max Ops life from Lizard. Obviously she was wrong. She dropped her gaze, and shrugged.

There was a long silence. Finally, she looked up at him. It was like looking at a jade wall. His jaw was clenched, and his eyes had a defensive wariness that she hadn't seen since the first time she met him.

'I knew this would happen one day,' said Lizard. 'People always let you down sooner or later. I've always wondered why you bothered with me. That's another secret I'll never know.' He shoved the book into his satchel and stood up. 'I'll do this myself. I don't need you.' He strode through the beaded curtain in the doorway and left.

Lili looked at his rigid back, but said nothing. For three years she had told no one about her Maximum Ops training. Nobody really cared what she did anyway, no one other than Lizard.

Lizard's footsteps thumped angrily all the way down the steps.

Lili knew she had to choose—her friendship

with Lizard, or her loyalty to Maximum Operations Enterprise. She went to the window and leaned out. Lizard was down below, kicking the concrete pillar outside the shop.

'*Wei*,' she called out.

Lizard stopped kicking.

'Well, come on, then!' she said and she went back inside and waited.

Lizard's fingers appeared a moment later, gripping the faded green windowsill. He pulled himself up and on to it. He squatted there, glowering like a gargoyle.

Lili stuck her head out through the beaded curtain and checked that there was no one on the landing outside the room. She came back in and sat down on the floor.

'Promise you won't tell anyone,' said Lili.

Still scowling, he nodded.

'Maximum Operations Enterprise,' she said.

'What?' Lizard came off the sill and sat down in front of her. And Lili told him everything about her mission and the importance of the codebook.

'Gosh,' said Lizard when she stopped talking. She was relieved to see the defensiveness gone from his face. He scratched his head. 'Maybe you shouldn't have told me *everything*.'

She rolled her eyes. 'Stupid boy,' she said in Cantonese.

Lizard grinned, but his grin faded, as he digested Lili's story. 'So, what are we going to do? We can't abandon Georgina. She really is in danger. They might ransom her for the codebook.'

'She's British, the daughter of an important British man. They won't hurt her,' Lili said dismissively.

'Are you sure?' asked Lizard.

Lili thought back to what Miss Neha and Miss Adelia had said. She thought about jealous, ambitious Japan and the smugly superior British and found she wasn't sure at all. It was her fault that Georgina had been kidnapped. If she had been focused on her mission and not distracted by Lizard, then she would have seen the man sneaking up and she could have stopped him. That Japanese spy wasn't the only one with poisoned darts.

Lizard's face was troubled. 'We have to rescue her,' he said.

'I suppose so,' Lili said, reluctantly. 'And the book. You understand that's crucial for all of us, right? I have to get the book to Maximum Ops.'

Lizard nodded. 'After we rescue Georgina,' he said stubbornly.

'All right,' said Lili. She would complete her task and return the codebook—it would just take a little longer than ideal.

Without knowing it, Lizard had interfered in an important covert mission. Maximum Ops might think he was stealing the codebook for the enemy. Lizard could end up in prison or worse, and Lili wasn't sure the authorities would listen to her—a girl, non-British, on her first mission. She made her mind up: her report would not mention Lizard. The important thing was getting the codebook— there was no need to drag Lizard into something that was likely to end badly for him.

'How are we going to find Georgina—and the book?' asked Lizard.

Just then, Ting Ha came in with Brylcreem.

'Hey, you two.' Ting Ha beamed. 'You know Brylcreem?'

'Uh,' Lizard said, rubbing his lip. 'Yes.'

Brylcreem sat down next to Lizard, giving him a gentle nudge in the arm.

'Sure, this my good friend, Lizard.' His eyes beseeched Lizard not to mention how he'd got his cut lip.

Lizard grinned. 'Yeah, we're great buddies,' he said. 'And this is Lili.'

'Hey, Ting Ha's cousin!' said Brylcreem with a big smile.

Lizard had an idea. 'Brylcreem, we've got a problem,' he said. 'Do you think you could help us?'

Lili shot him a ferocious glare.

Lizard ignored her. 'Someone's been kidnapped by a Japanese guy,' he said. 'From Raffles Hotel. Do you have any idea where she might be taken?'

'No problem for my Brylcreem, right?' boasted Ting Ha, giving his quiff a loving pat. 'He know all the Hokkien in Singapore. You help him pass the police exam and he help you.' She looked at Brylcreem. 'Right, honey?'

Instead of blushing or scowling in embarrassment at being called honey, Brylcreem grinned and said, 'Sure, honey.' He turned to Lizard. 'What happen?'

'He kidnapped a girl from Raffles Hotel this evening. She's only a kid. Her father's a big shot Englishman. He runs the New British East India Company,' Lizard said. 'She has wavy red hair and blue, blue eyes.'

'Why he do that?' asked Brylcreem, scratching his forehead.

'They want to ransom her for some information,' Lizard lied smoothly. Lili raised an eyebrow but said nothing. 'I think it's to do with the Japanese war in China. And I think maybe their war coming to Malaya and even Singapore.'

'The Japanese?' Ting Ha frowned. 'You know Boss Man Beng got killed yesterday? My uncle in the police, he say the knife is Japanese army type.'

Brylcreem nodded. 'And many Japanese shops are closing, because people not buying from them.'

'Really?' asked Lili. This was new, even though she knew that anti-Japanese feeling had been growing worse in Singapore recently.

'Kidnapping a girl, huh? That's bad,' Brylcreem said, shaking his head. 'A good fight between boys, no problem, but kidnapping girls is bad. All right, I go find out.'

'I hear the Japanese soldiers can be very cruel,' said Lizard.

'Oh, Brylcreem!' exclaimed Ting Ha. 'You must save her!' She wiped an angry tear away. 'You go now! Quick!'

'Don't worry, I fix it!' Brylcreem said, and he stood up with a noble squaring of his shoulders and then he swept out of the room. The effect was only slightly ruined by a crashing sound as he tripped over a stool. 'No problem here, no problem at all,' he called, and a faint stream of Hokkien swear words drifted down the stairs and out the door.

'What does red hair look like, huh?' mused Ting Ha.

'It's wavy. Like…waves. And shiny. With little

shiny gold bits,' said Lizard.

'*Wah!* Must be soft!' said Ting Ha.

'And clean. Smells so clean. And her eyes are blue like the sky when there are no clouds,' said Lizard.

'*Wah*, so nice, huh?' Ting Ha elbowed Lili.

Lili rolled her eyes. 'Got anything to eat? I'm hungry.'

Ting Ha bustled off to see what she could find.

CHAPTER NINE

The No-brain Street Brat

Lizard grinned smugly at Lili. 'So, what do you think? Wouldn't I make a great spy? And I didn't even say anything about your mission.'

Lili was impressed with how Lizard had got Brylcreem, with his wide Hokkien network, to search for Georgina, but she wasn't going to say so. 'Let me have the book again.' She stretched her hand out.

Lizard took it out of his satchel and gave it to her, and she studied the pages. It was obvious to Lili that it was indeed a codebook for turning messages into ciphers, or to decipher such codes.

Lizard noticed something had fallen out of the bag and onto the floor. He picked it up. It was some kind of blue, scrunched-up fabric, a little stiff. Lizard stared at it uncomprehendingly for a moment, then dropped it with a yelp.

Lili frowned at him.

'Look at that, Lili.' Lizard pointed to the fabric on the floor. 'Don't touch it. It's got Boss Man Beng's blood on it,' he said.

'What? What do you mean?'

'He grabbed my hand when he was…you know…'

'Dying?' asked Lili.

Lizard nodded.

'Boss Man Beng gave that to you when he was dying?' said Lili.

'I don't know if he meant to give it to me, but it was in his hand when he clutched mine, and I didn't even realise I had it until later,' said Lizard.

Lili picked it up and opened the fabric out. It was blue, with a hand-painted pattern of green bamboo on it. Dark brown blotches spoilt the beautiful pattern. 'It's a handkerchief. Look, you can see where it was folded.' She rubbed a stain-free corner between her fingers. 'It's silk.'

Lizard snorted. 'Boss Man would never carry a

silk handkerchief.'

'So whose is it, then?'

'Could it be the killer's?' Lizard gasped.

'My father used to sell silk handkerchiefs in his shop,' Lili said. 'He would make a suit and shirt for someone, and then sell them a silk handkerchief to finish the look. Mr Tanaka from Tanaka's Emporium delivered the silk.'

'I know that shop,' said Lizard. 'It's in Middle Road. It's built like a fortress. Three floors of grey concrete. It's nothing like the old shop houses next to it. It even has a lift!'

'I remember Father joking that the Japanese could withstand a siege in the emporium if they needed to,' Lili said. 'Not so funny now. People say a lot of the Japanese in Malaya are spies.'

They both stared at the handkerchief in Lili's hand.

'Wait a minute,' Lizard said slowly. 'Tanaka's Emporium is in Middle Road, and I was there today. I followed Katsu—you know, that spy—and then I lost him in Middle Road.'

'Built like a fortress…' Lili said, staring.

'A fortress can keep people out,' said Lizard.

'…or keep people in,' finished Lili.

'Georgina could be locked up in there,' said Lizard, standing up. 'We need to go there. Now.'

Lili sighed. She tucked the book and the handkerchief into the front of her tunic.

'Hey, you can't keep that book. I found it,' Lizard protested. He didn't seem to care so much about the blood-stained handkerchief.

'Stole it, you mean. I need the book, Lizard. We're going to look for the English girl now, because that's what you want, right?' Lili said. 'The book is important for stopping a war, and I need to get it to Maximum Operations. You need to trust me.'

'No,' he said flatly. 'There's a whole side of you I don't know. How can I trust you?'

Lili knew she could easily out-manoeuvre Lizard, tie him up, escape with the book and take it straight to Max Ops headquarters. She could have been halfway there already. That's what her S-Stream training told her to do. But if she did that, Lizard would never trust her again.

'Wait, let me think,' she said. 'Don't talk for a minute.'

Lizard kept silent as Lili propped her chin in her hand and stared out the window for five minutes.

'Got it,' she said at last. She went out onto the landing and came back with a lantern, which she put on the floor. She put her hand into one of her tunic pockets and took out something metal.

'What is that?' asked Lizard.

'Camera,' Lili said. It felt odd to openly use classified Maximum Ops technology in front of a civilian. She moved the book into the light and took a photo of the cover, then opened the book.

'Gosh! A tiny spy camera!' said Lizard. 'Terrific—can I try it?'

'It's not a toy, Lizard,' she snapped. 'Make yourself useful and turn the pages.'

Lizard threw her a wounded look, but Lili was too busy to notice. It took a while, but eventually they finished photographing all the pages of the book.

'All right,' said Lili, straightening up. 'Now we can use the book to get Georgina back.'

'But don't you need the book?' Lizard asked.

'Not now. I have all the information now.' She waved the little camera at him. 'And we need to give it back to the Japanese anyway. It is a codebook, Lizard. What would you do if you had a code that has been broken?'

'Um...not use it anymore?'

'Exactly. With any luck, they'll think we are just thieving children who don't know what we stole,' said Lili. 'They will want to believe it, too. After all, who wants to be the one to tell the Japanese Navy boss that they have to make a new code system? Just imagine. I think they'd get flogged until they were dead horses.'

Lizard shivered, thinking of the things Fatty Dim Sum had told him about Japanese soldiers. 'So we'll give them the book back?'

'Yes,' said Lili. 'And we'll tell them that Katsu dropped it!'

'But he didn't,' said Lizard, scratching his head.

'No, but we'll tell them you followed Katsu from Fatty Dim Sum's to Middle Road and that he dropped the book and you picked it up.' A small grin appeared on her face. 'Mix a little truth in with the big lie and they will believe it for sure.'

'But Katsu will deny it,' said Lizard.

'Yes, he will,' said Lili, nodding.

'And they'll think Katsu's a dirty double-crossing rat!' said Lizard, looking awed.

'Yes, they will,' Lili said grimly.

'Crumbs, I hope I'm never not on your side.'

'They'll think Katsu was going to sell it to the British, but he never got the chance,' said Lili. 'Then some no-brain street brat—that's you—picked it up, and they'll be happy that the British did not get it back. Now, you have to do exactly what I say, understand?'

'Who made you the boss?'

'Three years of Maximum Ops training,' she said, and she breezed out through the beaded curtain.

Just outside, they met Ting Ha coming towards them with a pile of curry puffs.

'Eh, you two. You like Nonya curry puff? I got you some…' she started.

'Nonya, Malay, Chinese, Indian—I've never met a curry puff I didn't like,' Lizard said with a grin.

'Thanks, Ting Ha,' Lili said, and took two as she went past.

'Marvellous,' said Lizard, as he grabbed two in each hand. 'Toodle pip!' He took a bite of one, and as always thought of Uncle Archie and wondered if they'd ever have curry puffs together again.

'Whaat?' Ting Ha said, turning to look at their backs. 'What you say? Where you going?'

'Out,' said Lizard in a muffled, crumbly voice and, in a flurry of thumping footsteps, they were gone.

'Those two crazy,' muttered Ting Ha. She took a bite out of the last curry puff and crumpled up the greasy paper wrapper.

CHAPTER TEN

Tanaka's Emporium

Lili and Lizard stepped out into the night-time hustle of Tanjong Pagar Road. Tanaka's Emporium was only a mile or two away, and the walk would give them time to work out a plan.

'Just a minute. I have to go back in,' said Lili.

'What for?' asked Lizard.

'To "spend the penny".' She waggled her eyebrows meaningfully.

'Oh. Hurry up, then,' he said and turned away.

Lili ran, not back up the stairs but into the shop and called to Ting Ha's ten-year-old brother, who was stacking tins in an aisle.

She checked that Lizard couldn't see her. 'Hey, Ah Di,' Lili said in Cantonese. She grabbed a pencil and a piece of paper from her pocket and wrote a message in a quick, simple code that she had learnt in an S-Stream codes and ciphers class. She gave Ting Ha's brother the message and a coin. 'Five cents to take this to Miss Neha at the Girls' Mission School. You know where that is, right?'

'Sure,' said the boy. 'Sophia Road. But so far, and uphill too…'

Lili dropped another coin into the boy's hand. 'All right, but make sure you hurry all the way. Tell Miss Neha I said you will get another five cents when she gets the message.'

The boy gave a grin that split his cheerful face in half and he ducked outside.

Lili watched him go with a few misgivings. She knew she was breaching Lizard's trust already, but rescuing the English girl would be dangerous— she wanted Maximum Ops back-up. She hurried back onto the street. 'All done. Let's go,' she said to Lizard.

Lizard, who had noted Ting Ha's little brother speeding past him a second ago, looked at Lili suspiciously.

'Where is Ting Ha's brother going in such a rush?' he asked.

'Hurry up,' Lili called over her shoulder as she strode past him and up the road. 'I think you should provide a distraction so that I can sneak in and find out if the English girl is really there.'

'And I'll ask for Mr Tanaka, give him the book and get Katsu into a whole lot of trouble,' said Lizard.

'Perfect,' said Lili.

When they got to Tanaka's Emporium, they were relieved to see that it was still open.

Lizard nodded at Lili, took a deep breath and opened the door. He saw Mr Tanaka frown as he went in.

'Excuse me, Mr Shinozaki,' Mr Tanaka said to the only other person Lizard could see in the shop. 'I will just close up, then we can talk.'

Lizard looked carefully at the other man and was relieved that he looked official, but not soldierly. The man had thick wire-rimmed spectacles and a little moustache.

'Sorry, shop closed now,' Mr Tanaka said to Lizard. 'Come back tomorrow.'

The shop had high ceilings and was surprisingly airy and elegant, despite its solid concrete exterior. Full-length glass cabinets filled with silks lined the walls. Lizard fixed his gaze above the cabinets in the back corner of the shop.

'*Wah*, very big rat up there.' Lizard pointed somewhere to Mr Tanaka's left.

Mr Tanaka looked. 'No rats here!' he exclaimed, outraged.

'There, there! Moving fast, what.' Lizard walked towards the back corner of the shop.

Even Mr Shinozaki followed Lizard and peered upwards.

'Oh,' Lizard said. 'Sorry, it's just a shadow, or something. Sorry.'

Mr Tanaka shook his head, irritated. 'Out now!' he said.

'But I must talk to you, Mr Tanaka,' Lizard said nervously. 'I found something. A Japanese book or something. It was dropped in the street.'

'What?' said Mr Tanaka, surprised.

Lizard opened his satchel and showed Mr Tanaka a corner of the book. Mr Shinozaki craned his neck to look too.

'A big Japanese man dropped it outside,' said Lizard, gulping. He took the book out of his bag.

'Oh,' Mr Tanaka stepped back. 'Nothing to do with me, but—I'll show it to someone. You stay here.'

He took the book from Lizard, and vanished through a doorway behind the counter.

'Boy,' said Mr Shinozaki. 'If you know what's good for you, you will leave now, and don't come back.' He put his hand in his pocket. 'Here.' He handed Lizard a note.

Lizard looked at it. King George's stern face glared at him from the note. One dollar.

'I can't,' said Lizard, holding the note back out to Mr Shinozaki.

'Keep it.' The man looked at him and sighed.

Mr Tanaka came back just as Lizard pocketed the dollar note.

'You come in,' he said to Lizard, now looking as

nervous as Lizard felt. 'Someone want to see you.'

'He's only a boy. He should go,' said Mr Shinozaki. He lowered his voice but Lizard could still hear him. 'He is too young to be here.'

'*He* want to talk to the boy now.' Mr Tanaka looked at Mr Shinozaki. 'What can we do?'

Mr Shinozaki said nothing for a moment. Then he straightened up. '*Hai*,' he said. 'I can see you will be busy. I will come back another time.' And he left the shop.

'Come, come,' said Mr Tanaka, looking wretched. 'Now you are here, you must come in.'

Lizard wanted to bolt from the shop like Mr Shinozaki had told him to, but he couldn't. Georgina had to be saved. He and Lili had a plan, and he needed to do his part. With a gulp, he followed Mr Tanaka into the back of the shop.

Lili crouched halfway up the stairs. Lizard had done well, distracting Mr Tanaka and that other man with his absurd rat story. As if any rodent would set paw in such a hygienic, crumb-free place. She crept silently up to the next floor and peered around the corner.

A young man stood, busy cutting some silk spread out on a big table. Fortunately, he had his back to her. He sang along to a Japanese song coming from a radio in a corner of the large room. Bolts of fabric and boxes were stacked up beyond him, and furniture was pushed against the wall. It all looked very crowded, as if the space wasn't supposed to have this much in it—perhaps it had all been moved here to make room elsewhere.

This was a three-storey building. Perhaps room had been made for a prisoner on the topmost floor?

Lili had to get past the man cutting silk at the table. She sprinted as lightly as she could past him and up the stairs. As she crouched out of sight, she was horrified to hear the man stop singing.

'*Hai*?' he shouted.

Lili could hear someone yelling for him from the ground floor. The man stomped downstairs, and Lili shivered at the thought of what would have happened if she had been caught.

She looked around the landing of the topmost

floor and saw a closed door to her left.

Cautiously, she turned the handle. To her surprise, the door opened. Inside was a stockroom, with boxes and bolts of fabric stacked against the wall. Ahead of her was a cage with steel bars. A girl knelt inside it, fiddling with the padlock.

It was Georgina Whitford Jones. She was so busy with the lock that she hadn't even noticed Lili come in.

Lili took in the sweaty, red, scowling face with matching gingery hair stuck in damp tendrils on her cheeks and forehead. The girl gave little grunts of concentration while she worked the lock with a hairpin.

Take the English princess out of the lavish surroundings of a Raffles suite and a sweaty mess was what you got, thought Lili. But she felt a begrudging admiration creep over her. At least Georgina was working hard with a cleverly improvised tool, and not curled up in a corner blubbing for her father.

'Hey,' Lili whispered.

Georgina jerked back, startled.

'Shh,' said Lili, putting her finger to her lips. She moved to the cage.

'Who are you?' Georgina whispered, her eyes wide. They really were like the sky on a cloudless day, thought Lili. She tried not to stare, but she had never seen eyes so blue.

'I'm here to get you out,' Lili said. 'Give me that hairpin.' Lili wished she had brought her lock-picking tool, with its choice of metal picks in several shapes and sizes.

'Here,' said Georgina, passing it over. 'I've been trying for ages. It looked so easy in the *Schoolgirls' Own Annual* escapology feature.'

'Some locks arc harder than others,' Lili said. 'And it's never easy with just a hairpin.'

Georgina watched Lili work at the lock. 'Who are you? Did my father send you? How—'

'Quiet. I need to concentrate,' Lili said.

The lock looked like a five-pin tumbler, possible to pick with a hairpin, but she had to get the tension just right...

CHAPTER ELEVEN

The Cage

Lizard followed Mr Tanaka into the back of the shop and along a passageway to a closed door. Mr Tanaka opened it and gestured for Lizard to go in.

'Are you coming?' Lizard asked. The man wasn't a friend, but he was a familiar face.

Mr Tanaka shook his head without meeting Lizard's eye and shut the door gently after him. Lizard stood inside the room, heart pounding, staring at the door and willing it to open again.

'Turn around, boy,' said a gruff voice behind him.

Lizard jumped in fright. He took a deep breath and turned. A man wearing a hood covering his head stood in the shadows. Lizard was bewildered for a moment and then relieved—the man wanted to keep his identity secret and Lizard was fine with that. It gave him hope that he might be allowed to leave later on.

'Where did you get this?' the man said, holding up the codebook. He had only a slight Japanese accent and Lizard got the feeling he was disguising his voice.

'The man—tall fellow—he dropped it,' Lizard said. He heard his voice wavering. *Pull yourself together*, he told himself.

'Where did you see him?'

'He was in Fatty Dim Sum's coffee shop this afternoon,' said Lizard. 'He chased me but I got away. Then I saw him go past the market and I followed him to Middle Road right outside this shop. He dodged to avoid a bicycle and the book fell out of his pocket.'

'Why didn't you bring it here straight away?' asked the hooded man.

Steady, Lizard said to himself. *Stick to the story we prepared*. 'I wanted to see if I could sell it,' he said. 'But when I looked in it, I couldn't understand it. Nobody I know would buy it, so I thought if I brought it back maybe I could get…a reward…' His voice trailed off.

Unexpectedly, the man laughed. 'Yes, this I can believe, young man! Did you show it to anyone?'

'No,' said Lizard, feigning disgust. 'I was going to throw it away but then I thought maybe the man might want it back. Maybe he would give me money for it.'

'The man,' said the hooded man. 'Would you recognise him again?'

'Yes. He was taller and uglier than everybody else,' said Lizard.

The hooded man turned and opened a door next to him. He spoke in Japanese with someone outside. Lizard heard the words 'Katsu' and '*hai*' several times. He turned back to Lizard.

'Now, we shall see,' the man said grimly, folding his arms.

Lizard stared at the floor and waited for what felt like a very long time.

Finally the door opened again. Lizard saw Katsu being dragged in by two other men.

'Is this the man who dropped the book?' the hooded man asked.

Lizard nodded.

'He's lying!' Katsu shouted and he lunged at Lizard.

Lizard stumbled back, startled, and the hooded man barked an order to his men.

The men held Katsu tight. Katsu struggled, but then one of the men pulled out a gun and cocked it with the loudest click in the world. Lizard was horrified. He'd never seen a gun up close before. Knives, yes, plenty, but not a gun.

'I didn't do whatever this dirty animal said I did!' Katsu said, breathing heavily.

Lizard looked at Katsu's face, screwed up with bitter hostility. He was stunned at the effects of his lie.

'Whatever he said, it's not true! He's making it up! How can you believe this worthless brat over me?' Katsu lunged at Lizard again, and the men nearly lost their hold on him. The man with the gun jammed it against Katsu's temple.

Lizard was drenched with icy sweat in dread of the gun firing.

The hooded man turned to Lizard, his head tilted as if thinking things over. 'No. It is not possible for an ignorant boy like him to make such a story up. It would take too much knowledge, too much planning, for little gain. And how would he have got the book otherwise?'

'*He* must have stolen it!' snarled Katsu.

Lizard quaked, for of course Katsu was right.

'Impossible.' The hooded man turned again to Lizard. 'Are you sure this is the man who dropped the book?'

Part of Lizard's brain screamed *No! Let him go*, but the other part said, *It's him or me. And Lili. He probably killed Boss Man Beng.*

Lizard gulped, dropped his eyes, and nodded once, slowly.

The hooded man sighed. 'How much did you think you would get from the British, Katsu?' He turned to the man with the gun. 'Take him away.'

'He's lying!' Katsu's face was purple now. His

maddened eyes bored into Lizard's. 'How can you do this to me? I'll get you, you filthy liar! I will *destroy* you!'

As the men wrenched him towards the door, Katsu spat at Lizard and got him full in the face. It burned like acid.

The door slammed shut after them.

Lizard could hear Katsu screaming his innocence. He wiped the spit off his face, guilt and horror twisting his heart.

'You won't...shoot him, will you?' Lizard whispered.

'Why do you care?' said the hooded man.

Lizard was silent. Then he said, 'Can I go now?'

'You haven't asked for your reward yet,' said the hooded man, a sarcastic sneer in his voice.

'I just want to go.' Lizard stared at the floor.

'I don't think I will let you go just yet. Not until I'm sure,' said the hooded man. 'Come, let's go upstairs. And if you are thinking about trying to get away, let me just inform you, I too have a gun.'

The man opened the door, gave a bow and swept

his right hand in front of him to bid Lizard go ahead. They went up to the top floor. Lizard was relieved to see Georgina. She was in a cage, sweaty and tousled, but she was unhurt. She gasped when she saw Lizard, but she didn't say anything.

'Children! Why am I suddenly infested with children?' the hooded man muttered, as he unlocked the cage door and pushed Lizard in. 'Stay there and be quiet until I decide what to do with you.' Then he locked the cage and left, closing the door behind him.

'Dinesh!' Georgina said, when the man had gone.

'Missy! Are you all right?' Lizard said. He was relieved to see her, though she was so dishevelled he almost didn't recognise her.

'Get me out of this cage!' she hissed furiously. Her sweaty face was nearly as red as her hair.

'Why do you call him Dinesh?' asked Lili, slipping out from behind some boxes. She glared at Georgina.

Lizard jumped. '*Aiyah*, you!' he exclaimed. 'Don't sneak up like that!'

Georgina looked at Lili and put her hand on

Lizard's arm. 'I don't believe we've been formally introduced. Dinesh, dear, would you please do the honours?'

Lili looked at Georgina's hand on Lizard's arm, and her lips tightened.

'Uh…Missy Georgina, this is Lili. Lili, this is Missy Georgina,' Lizard said miserably. He wasn't sure why, but there was more hostility in the room now than there was when the hooded man had been here.

'So pleased to meet you,' Georgina smiled sweetly at Lili, then turned to Lizard. 'Dinesh, surely *you* can get me out of here?'

'Ah,' said Lizard, all too aware of Georgina's hand on his sweaty forearm. 'Yes?' He looked at Lili, knowing that only Lili could unlock the cage.

Lili rolled her eyes. She knelt down and started to pick at the lock again. 'What happened?' she asked.

Lizard told her about the hooded man and Katsu, guilt still raw in his chest. 'Do you think they'll shoot him?' he said to Lili.

'You did what you had to do, Lizard. Don't

worry about Katsu, because right now we should be worrying about whether they are going to shoot *us*.'

Georgina's eyes were wide. 'What's going on? Why did they kidnap me?'

'Because...' Lizard started.

'You don't need to know,' Lili interrupted, looking up from the lock to glare at Georgina through the bars.

'Yes, I do need to know! It's to do with that book you stole from my father, isn't it? They asked me about it, but I only said that I had found it in the hotel. I didn't say anything about you.' She looked at Lizard. 'I demand that you tell me everything!'

'Yes, Missy,' Lili said, her eyes cold. 'I tell you what you want to know. Bad Japanese soldiers kidnap you for *cheen*.'

'What's *cheen*?' asked Georgina, wrinkling her nose.

'Money,' Lizard said.

'If you allow, your highness, I'll get back to work now, getting you two out of this cage.' Lili looked down at the lock. 'You can demand all you like once we've escaped.'

Georgina's glare was like a tribal ritual mask, but she didn't argue.

Lizard could see that she was saving it for later. 'Hush!' he said. 'Do you hear that? I think someone's coming.'

Lili slipped behind the boxes again.

Boots clomped to the door, and it swung open to reveal one of the Japanese men, holding a large jug.

He unlocked the cage door and put the jug on the floor inside, then he locked up and clomped out again, without a single word.

Lizard was grateful as he saw what was in the jug. 'Water,' he said as Lili came out again.

'That's good, isn't it?' Georgina asked, with just a small tremble in her voice. 'They wouldn't give us water if they were going to…'

Lili glanced at Georgina. 'Here,' she said gruffly. 'You better drink now.'

Georgina and Lizard drank, then poured some water through the bars into Lili's cupped hands. Lili drank too, then went back to working at the lock with Georgina's hairpins.

The heat was stifling. Sweat trickled down Lizard's face, no matter how often he wiped it. He wished he could take off his shirt, but Georgina's presence made that unthinkable.

Lizard and Georgina watched in silence as Lili make the tiniest movements in the lock with the hairpin. Their fear gave way to boredom as time dragged by.

Lili was too busy thinking to be bored. As her hands got on with the task of picking the lock, her brain was analysing their situation. The hooded man and his thugs were obviously part of a well-organised group. In spite of their civilian clothes, everything about their behaviour, the way they stood, even their haircuts, announced one thing to Lili: gunjin. Spying gunjin.

She remembered something she had seen two months ago, when Miss Adelia had taken the S-Stream girls to Fort Canning Hill to observe the layout of the town and the harbour. While all the other visitors had been looking at the pretty view of the sea, three Japanese men dressed in suits were only interested in the covered water reservoir to their right. Lili's Japanese was good enough for her to pick up that the men were discussing the water supply. One of them took photographs of the reservoir. At the time Lili thought they must have been engineers or fanatical reservoir hobbyists. But now she had other thoughts.

Lili had been trained to notice things and she had noticed those men. She understood now that they had been planning for war. War in Singapore. Invading armies need water, so best not to damage the water supply. Why hadn't she alerted Miss Adelia? That was as bad as not noticing in the first place.

What could damage a concrete-covered reservoir? Tanks? Bombs? Lili shivered at the thought of tanks and bombs in Singapore.

'Dinesh,' Georgina whispered. 'Can you at least tell me where we are?'

'We're in Tanaka's Emporium, in Middle Road. It sells silk cloth and stuff like that,' Lizard whispered to Georgina.

'Well, isn't that just too funny,' said Georgina, not looking amused at all.

'Why?' asked Lizard.

Georgina pointed to the boxes next to the cage. Lizard peered at them. Two of them had *New British East India Co.* stamped on them.

'That's the company my father works for,' she said. 'It exports silks and other things from India.'

'Oh,' said Lizard.

'Anyway, that's not important,' Georgina said. 'The Japanese—they kidnapped me because of that book, didn't they? The one with the strange writing. It's Japanese, isn't it?'

Lizard nodded.

'Do you know what it is?' she asked.

Lili gave him a warning glance, and Lizard shook his head.

Georgina frowned at Lizard. 'Well, tell me how you met *her*, then.' She tilted her head at Lili.

Lizard gave a soft laugh. 'She caught me stealing from her cousin.'

'Oh!' Georgina's eyes opened wide. 'Then she

had you arrested?'

'No. Then she bought me a plate of fried noodles.' He grinned.

'But why...' Georgina started.

'Stop asking so many questions!' Lili said suddenly, her eyes lifting to catch Georgina's. 'Don't you understand? You're not our *friend.*'

Georgina stared back, genuine astonishment and dismay on her face. 'Don't *you* understand?' she said. 'I know those thugs might kill me and I need...'

'Ah! Got it!' said Lili in triumph and she swung the cage door open. 'Quick, let's go. Through the window over there, behind those rolls of silk. We'll have to move them out of the way *quietly.*'

Lizard and Georgina got up, stiff from being still for so long, and began lifting the long bolts of silk stacked upright in front of the window and lying them down against the door.

'Wait!' said Georgina, stopping still. 'I can hear something. They're coming back!'

Sure enough, Lili felt the vibrations through the wooden floors, vibrations that she knew would soon turn into the familiar thump of heavy boots.

'To blazes with quietly!' Lizard dropped the bolt he was carrying. 'Get them all out of the way now!'

They scrambled to the window, and Lili pushed the remaining rolls aside and swept back the curtains. The thud of boots got louder and louder.

They all looked at the window. It was open, but it was barred. Lili grasped the bars and tried to shake them, but it was no use. They were still trapped.

'No!' Lili gasped, just as the boots clomped to a stop outside, and the door handle turned.

CHAPTER TWELVE

A Bullet Hole

There was a grunt of surprise as the door met resistance from the bolts of silk on the floor. Then the door was shoved open and Lizard was alarmed to recognise the man in the doorway as the one who had put the gun to Katsu's head.

He was not as big as Katsu, but his closely shaved head made him resemble him so much that Lizard found himself thinking of him as Little Katsu. The man stood there, staring at the empty cage and then at the three by the window until he recovered and yelled something over his shoulder.

He turned back to look at them. 'How you get out?' he said.

More loud steps thumped up the stairs, and the hooded man appeared in the doorway. He pointed at

Lili. 'You! Who are you? How did you get in here?'
He moved towards her menacingly.

Lizard jumped in front of Lili. 'Run!' he gasped,
pointing at the door.

Lili dodged Lizard and snap-kicked Little Katsu
in the stomach.

'*Oof!*' he grunted and grabbed at her, missing.

Lili swung round with a sweeping kick and
smacked Little Katsu in the face with her foot. He
stumbled back and tripped over a bolt of silk, falling
heavily on his back. Boxes crashed to the floor.

Georgina jumped over the bolts and headed
for the door, but the hooded man was in her way,
and she stopped short. In a split second she picked
up a skinny roll of silk and rammed it hard into his
stomach. The hooded man doubled over. Georgina
dropped the bolt and ran past him, but his arm shot
out and he grabbed her around the waist, shoving her
back into the room. The bolt she had dropped rolled
under her foot and she tripped and fell. She sat there,
gasping.

Meanwhile, Lizard had picked up a box and

smashed it over Little Katsu's head. Dozens of colourful reels of cotton burst out and clattered across the floor. Little Katsu rose up with the inevitability of a tidal wave, and reached out for Lizard.

'You dirty animal!' he snarled, grabbing Lizard by his shirt front. He shook Lizard until the little bones in his ears rattled.

Lizard was terrified. He knew this man could snap his neck as easily as a used satay stick if he wanted to, and he was pretty sure he wanted to.

'Let him go!' shouted Lili, as a loud blast shook the room. She turned to see the hooded man pointing a smoking hand gun at the ceiling and a newly created bullet hole in the plaster above him.

'Amusing as it is to watch Nobu fighting little children, I must insist you all stop,' said the hooded man. He dipped at the waist, and stretched his hand, gun still in it, towards the cage in a mock gesture of invitation. 'Please enter this humble abode.'

Little Katsu, whose name was actually Nobu, flung Lizard into the cage. Then he seized Lili and pushed her in. Georgina, not wanting to be touched by the brute, stumbled in by herself.

Lizard lay on the floor, stunned and breathless. He was shocked at how quickly the rescue had become a disaster. Their secret weapon, ace girl spy Lili, had turned out to be no match for these gunjin thugs.

Nobu slammed the cage door shut, took a ring of keys out of his pocket and locked the padlock.

'Now this is an interesting situation,' said the hooded man, putting his gun back in its holster and pulling his jacket flap over it. 'Who are you, little girl, and how did you children manage to unlock the cage and make such a terrible mess in here?'

'I come before,' said Lili, putting on a street accent. 'I want get...money...I hide. Wait for everybody go home.'

Lizard was impressed that Lili hadn't given up. Maybe things weren't totally hopeless just yet.

'Indeed?' said the hooded man, sounding sceptical. 'And how did you open the cage?'

There was a silence.

Nobu whacked the cage bars with his ring of

keys, making everyone jump back. 'Talk!' he yelled.

They flinched. Georgina stood taller, took a deep breath and moved to the front of the cage. 'I demand you let us go!' she said, her voice quavering.

The hooded man moved forward. 'You do, do you?' He stared in through the bars at her. 'Well I am not your subject, to order around as you please. You British! The people of Asia are finished with being slaves to the British. I tell you, Malaya and especially Singapore will be better with new masters. Why should the British take all the best parts of the world? Asia should be ruled by Asia's people. We Japanese will expand our empire and make Asia supreme!'

Lizard's mind flashed back to what Fatty Dim Sum had said to him at the wet market. He sat up. 'The British aren't cruel to the Chinese,' he said.

'Yes, they are,' the hooded man said. 'Unfortunate things happen in a war, but the British—even in peace time their razors slice sharp and slow, so you don't even know when you bleed.'

'You're mad!' Georgina said, her voice trembling.

'You British rob these people and you don't even

know it,' the hooded man said.

Even through the hood, his contempt for Georgina was obvious. He straightened and dusted himself off. 'It does not matter. I have what I need now, and I must get rid of you. Nobody important will miss you two,' he gestured at Lizard and Lili. 'And, as for you,' he looked at Georgina. 'There will be trouble, but I cannot have you running loose and telling tales.'

He barked something in Japanese to Nobu.

'*Hai*!' Nobu said, and he put his keys away and picked up a bolt of cream silk patterned with red and gold chrysanthemums and tore three long strips off it.

Lizard gulped. 'What are you doing?'

Nobu nodded respectfully towards the hooded man who was still standing at the door. 'I tie so you cannot see.' He held up the three strips of silk. 'Who is first?'

There was a knocking sound from outside the room. The hooded man turned, and went out onto the landing. Suddenly, a hand reached out and yanked him out of view.

Nobu dropped the three pieces of silk. They fluttered as they fell: cream, gold, red. Before they touched the floor, a yell tore through the air. A herd of teenage boys pounded into the room, knocking Nobu down.

One of the boys came to a halt in front of the cage. Lizard looked up into the grinning face of Brylcreem. He was waving the hooded man's gun. Lizard had never been so glad to see anybody in his life.

CHAPTER THIRTEEN

Does Silk Make Noise?

Lizard looked past Brylcreem and saw Buck Tooth and a gang of teenage boys all carrying makeshift weapons and yelling threats in Hokkien. They piled on top of Nobu, who struggled, but he was outnumbered. In a few moments he was lying face-down, his arms twisted up his back, with four boys sitting on him.

Lizard vowed to teach Brylcreem so much English that he'd pass the police proficiency test as easy as coconut pie.

'Quiet!' yelled Brylcreem.

The noise settled, and Brylcreem peered through the bars of the cage. '*Wei*, you all right?' he asked them.

Lili pointed at Nobu. 'He's got the keys. Get us out!'

Brylcreem bent over the man and rummaged in his pockets. He found the keys and a moment later Lizard, Lili and Georgina were out of the cage. Brylcreem gave Lizard a quick manly hug and patted Lili on the shoulder. He nodded at Georgina.

'You kids all fine, huh?' he said.

'How did you find us?' said Lili.

'I didn't know you two'—he pointed at Lizard and Lili—'would be here. I came to find the English girl.'

'But how did you know?' said Lizard.

'I go see the boys gambling in Smith Street, ask if anything strange happening with the Japanese,' said Brylcreem. 'Ah Keung, he say his brother selling *poh piah* in Middle Road, see funny things sometimes at night here. Big boxes with animals or something going in the back alley. To a silk shop? He think it's strange.'

'Yes!' exclaimed Georgina. 'They put a horrid sack right over my head! I couldn't breathe!'

'Hey, Brylcreem!' yelled one of the boys sitting on Nobu. 'What we do with this bad guy?'

Brylcreem looked at Lizard, who jerked his head at the cage. 'Let's see how Nobu likes being locked up.'

The boys dragged Nobu into the cage. Brylcreem locked the door and tossed the keys to Lizard.

Nobu staggered to his feet and rushed to the bars, simmering with rage and shouting in Japanese.

Brylcreem reached between the bars and poked the man's forehead with a forceful finger. 'Quiet! Don't make me come in there and tie your mouth up!' He turned to Lizard. 'See? Must be tough with bad guys. I can be a good policeman, right?'

'Wait, where's the hooded man?' asked Lizard, anxiety flooding through him. The man was like a crocodile in a murky river, cunning and ruthless, and Lizard feared and respected him. Especially when he couldn't see him.

'Don't worry, I left Ah Kit and Ah Yan guarding him,' Brylcreem said, heading out of the room.

Out on the landing, Ah Kit and Ah Yan were sprawled on top of each other, unconscious, and the hooded man was nowhere to be seen.

'*Aiyah!*' yelled Brylcreem. He called the boys something rude in Hokkien and kicked them. They stirred, groaned and sat up. 'What kind of kung fu boys you call yourselves? Useless! You let that fellow get away, ah?'

'Let's get out of here,' said Lizard, relieved that the hooded man had gone, but afraid that he would return any minute with reinforcements. 'What happened to the other men?'

'What men?' said Brylcreem as they all trooped down the two flights of stairs. 'There was nobody else down there.'

Lili said nothing as they went into the airy shop. She was sure the hooded man was part of a secret organisation of Japanese spies that was gathering intelligence in preparation for war. She needed to tell Miss Adelia, but perhaps there was more information to find here first.

'Here,' said Brylcreem, reaching into a glass jar of lollies he'd found on one of the counters in the shop and giving handfuls of sweets to the boys. 'Thanks, huh?'

The boys took the lollies and whooped jubilantly. As far as they were concerned, they had beaten the bad guys and rescued a missy in distress; a *British* missy, what's more.

Lili ignored them and went into the back of the shop. 'Look,' she said, as Lizard joined her. She pointed to a metal lattice grill across a doorway. There was a cupboard-sized room beyond it.

'It's a lift,' said Georgina. 'Haven't you ever seen one? All the best department stores in London have them.'

'Yes, I know. They have them at the Capitol Theatre,' said Lizard proudly.

'Ah Keung's brother say a big wood box come in yesterday,' said Brylcreem. 'He think some animal in there, because it make some noise.'

'Really?' said Lili. 'What sort of noise?'

'Noise, *lah*!' said Brylcreem impatiently. 'Who care what noise? Does silk make noise?'

'Good point,' said Lili. If it wasn't silk, what was it? She had to find out, but not with Brylcreem's gang and Georgina there.

'Can you take Missy Georgina back to Raffles Hotel?' she asked Brylcreem. 'Just push her in the front door and they can give her back to her family,' she said. 'But go slowly, no need to rush.' Lili knew that as soon as Georgina arrived at Raffles, she would tell her parents where she had been and the police would come straight away. Lili needed time to gather some intelligence of her own.

'Why you not come?' said Brylcreem.

'Yeah, why?' said Lizard.

Lili frowned meaningfully at him. *I'm in charge*, said the look, *and don't forget it.*

Lizard grudgingly stopped talking.

'All right,' said Brylcreem, eyeing the lift. 'But don't go in there. I don't trust that thing. Come on, boys, let's go.' He gestured politely for Georgina to go ahead. 'We get a rickshaw for you, Missy.'

'But—' said Georgina, looking at Lizard.

Lizard opened his mouth to speak, but Lili got in first. 'You want to be locked back in that cage? I'm sure Nobu will make room for you. When the other thugs come back, you can all have tea and small

173

sandwiches together,' said Lili, her hand on her hip.

'You'll be all right,' said Lizard. 'Brylcreem's going to be a policeman. You'll be safer with him than anyone else in Singapore.'

Brylcreem grinned. 'You go Raffles, no trouble, I make sure, Missy.'

'Just think, iced drinks and electric fans,' Lili called as Georgina left with her troop of bodyguards.

Lizard was keen to leave too. He glanced round to make sure that he and Lili were alone in the shop. 'Why are we hanging around? Georgina is safe, and you've photographed the codebook,' he said.

'That doesn't mean we can't find out more about the book, and about what these spies are up to,' said Lili.

'You think we might find some clues?' said Lizard, a tiny hope flickering to life—maybe there was something to find out about Uncle Archie here.

'I'll never get another chance like this,' said Lili. 'Give me the keys.'

In a few moments, she had unlocked the metal grill door to the lift. Inside, there was a panel with buttons on it and she pressed the lowest one. With a clunk and a jerk, the small room moved downwards.

'The gunjin could be back any minute,' Lizard said nervously.

'We had better be quick, then,' said Lili, as the lift lurched to a stop. Lizard peered through the grill door, half expecting to see a grim gunjin staring at him, but there was no one there. He pulled open the door and they stepped into a gloomy basement. A single dim globe threw a little light onto a desk, but everything else was in shadows. Three desk drawers were open and empty, as if they had been cleared out in a hurry.

'Nothing,' Lili said in disgust. 'Looks like they took everything.'

'Not everything. Look at this,' said Lizard, crouching to pick up an envelope from under the desk. There was no letter inside, but the back of the envelope was covered in numbers. The numbers were in groups of five digits.

'Excellent,' said Lili, looking pleased as she tucked the envelope into her tunic. She found a light switch by the door and turned it on.

Lizard blinked in the glare of the main light. There was a cage in the shadows at the back of the room, just like the one upstairs.

Someone was sitting slumped in a chair in the corner of it.

Lili and Lizard approached cautiously. 'Hello?' said Lili.

No response.

'Hello?' she said again, louder.

The figure didn't move.

Now they could see that it was a man and that he was chained to the chair. He looked to be tall and he had limp, brownish hair. Lizard stepped right up to the cage. His hands reached up to grip the bars.

'Hello?' he whispered. His hands were sweaty on the bars.

The man slowly lifted his head.

'Hello?' Lizard whispered again, his heart beating so fast that it was like a trapped bird in his chest. He pressed against the bars, wanting them to dissolve, *willing* them to dissolve.

The man raised his eyes, and slowly focused on Lizard.

Lizard stared in at him. The face was haggard and exhausted.

And familiar.

'Uncle Archie?' Lizard's voice had a break in it.

'Lizard?' croaked the man. 'Is that really you?'

'Uncle Archie!' Lizard shook the bars, rattling the cage.

Lili's eyes widened in astonishment, and then she flicked through the keys in her hands. She found the right one and unlocked the cage door.

Lizard pushed past her and threw his arms around the dishevelled man. He squashed his face into his uncle's chest and hugged him hard.

'I've found you, Uncle Archie,' Lizard's voice was muffled against his uncle's chest. 'I can't believe I've finally found you.'

Lizard was almost afraid to open his eyes in case it was just another dream from which he'd wake and find Uncle Archie still missing. He had been waiting for Uncle Archie to come back to him every single moment, waking or sleeping, for the past two years.

'How can you possibly be here?' Uncle Archie said. He pressed his face into the top of Lizard's head. 'You've grown so much. I've *missed* you so much. I'm so sorry I couldn't get home to you—' His voice broke off.

Lizard lifted his face to his uncle's. 'What have they done to you?' he gasped in dismay, fully taking in Uncle Archie's bruised and gaunt face.

For a moment, the man's brow uncreased as he looked at Lizard. 'I'm all right, Lizard. Are *you* well, my boy?' he said. 'Did Pak Tuah look after you? Tell me.'

'Yes, yes, I'm fine. But—don't ever leave again, Uncle Archie,' said Lizard.

Uncle Archie's eyes filled with love and sadness, and Lizard knew he wouldn't make a promise he might not be able to keep.

Lizard turned to Lili. 'Let's get him out!'

But Uncle Archie was not only chained to the chair, but also to the solid iron bars behind him. Lili started trying the keys, one after the other, in the heavy padlock that secured the chain.

Uncle Archie stared at Lizard, suddenly intense. 'Lizard, there isn't much time. You must pass on a message for me,' he said. 'It's vitally important. I'm trusting you, my boy. You must go to Mr Davis at the Hill Street Export Offices and tell him that the gamekeeper says that autumn is coming so get marmalade.'

Lili shot a startled glance at Uncle Archie but didn't stop working at the lock.

'What? I don't understand,' Lizard said, bewildered.

Uncle Archie stared into his eyes, the way Lizard remembered he had always done when he needed Lizard to do something important. 'I know you don't understand,' said Uncle Archie, 'but you must trust me. Say it after me, Lizard. Tell Mr Davis that the gamekeeper says that autumn is coming so get marmalade.' Uncle Archie paused, waiting for Lizard to speak.

'Uh—go to Mr Davis,' replied Lizard.

Uncle Archie nodded. 'And tell him—'

'The gamekeeper says autumn is coming so get marmalade.'

'Well done, Lizard,' said Uncle Archie. Then he looked at both Lili and Lizard. 'You must not tell anyone but Mr Davis, understand?'

Lizard nodded, but Lili didn't.

'The teak box, Uncle Archie!' Lizard said. 'With the codebook—was it you? Did you get it from the Japanese?'

Uncle Archie stared at Lizard, eyes glinting. 'A codebook? What do you know about a codebook?'

'I...' Lizard didn't want to say the words 'stole it', nor could he ever lie to Uncle Archie. 'I got it from Raffles. I recognised the knot of the week. It was the Zeppelin, and it was tied with parachute cord just like we always practised tying knots with on the beach.'

Uncle Archie said nothing, but his eyes shone with pride, and he swallowed a lump in his throat.

'Well, what a coincidence, Lizard,' he said at last, a ghost of a smile breaking through the pain on his face. 'Just a coincidence, all right?'

Just then, they heard a clanking noise which

made them all jump. It was the lift, moving upwards. It clunked to a stop somewhere above them, and they could hear footsteps moving into it.

'None of these keys fit!' Lili burst out in frustration.

'Leave it and hide behind those crates,' Uncle Archie said. 'They mustn't see you! Lock the cage!'

The lift began its noisy descent as Lizard scrambled behind the crates and Lili locked the cage. She crouched down next to Lizard as the lift stopped, and they heard the grill slide open and footsteps move into the room.

Lizard peeked out from behind the crates and saw a person move towards the cage. She was impeccably dressed in a daisy-patterned frock with a smart pale blue handbag on her arm. Her silver hair caught the light. What could a well-dressed European lady possibly be doing here? thought Lizard.

'Miss Adelia!' Lili cried and burst out from behind the crates.

'Lili?' The lady turned a startled face to her.

'We have to get him out!' Lili cried, pointing into

the cage, and she hurried over with the keys in her hand. 'It's Lizard's uncle. Uncle Archie!'

Miss Adelia looked at the man, who was now sitting up straight and watching her.

'Madam, we don't have much time,' said Uncle Archie.

'Who are you?' Miss Adelia said. She glanced at Lili, who was unlocking the cage door.

'Please listen, they'll be back soon,' said Uncle Archie. 'You must ask for Mr Davis at the Hill Street Export Offices.'

Miss Adelia gave an involuntary blink. She leaned down and stared closer at Uncle Archie's face.

'Tell Mr Davis that Tanaka—he owns this shop— must be interviewed,' he said. 'Do you need to write this down?'

'I assure you my memory is excellent,' Miss Adelia said, as Lili swung the door open. Lizard dashed in again and gripped his uncle's shoulder. Lili handed the keys to Miss Adelia, who took them calmly and quickly tried the keys in the padlock on Uncle Archie's chains.

'When you go to Mr Davis, take the boy,' he said, nodding at Lizard. 'It's important.'

'What else can you tell me?' said Miss Adelia as she continued to test each key in the padlock.

'It's no use. Only the hooded man has the key to this padlock,' Uncle Archie said grimly.

'Look for tools,' Miss Adelia muttered to Lili.

Lili scrambled out and started searching the room for cutters or pliers.

There was a muffled thud from upstairs. This time, it had to be the gunjin returning for sure.

'Go now, behind that big crate there,' Uncle Archie lifted his chin towards it. 'There's a door. One of your keys will get you out.'

Miss Adelia rose without another word and strode behind the crate.

They could hear the grind of the lift now, and Japanese voices getting nearer all the time.

Lili dashed into the cage, grabbed Lizard and dragged him out.

'We can't just leave you!' Lizard gasped to his uncle.

'You must go. I'm happy you're in good hands,' Uncle Archie said. 'Get out of here, quick!'

The lift ground to a halt.

'We'll come back for you,' said Lili as she headed towards the big crate, holding on to Lizard's wrist as she went.

The lift grills clanked open.

'What? No!' Lizard started as Lili pulled him, staggering, behind her.

The hooded man rushed out, with three men close behind him.

'*No!*' Lizard shouted.

Uncle Archie didn't turn to look at the men. His eyes followed Lizard as Lili pulled him across the room.

The hooded man stopped still as his men ran past him. He glanced at Uncle Archie, then at Lizard, and he tilted his head as if puzzled as he watched Lizard vanish behind the crate.

Miss Adelia had opened the door, and Lili hauled Lizard through it, slamming it behind them. Miss Adelia was already halfway up a short flight of wooden stairs.

'Uncle Archie! We can't leave him,' Lizard yelled, shoving Lili aside and rattling the doorknob, but it had locked and was immoveable. Uncle Archie was cut off from him again.

'No!' he cried again, thumping the door hard with both fists.

Loud boot steps thundered on the other side, interspersed with shouts.

Lizard stared at the door, his hands clenched and white-knuckled against it. His head dropped onto his fists. Every muscle of his body was taut with despair and his breath came in short, agonised jerks. He didn't even flinch as a heavy boot kicked the door from the other side.

'*Kagi! Kagi!*' a voice yelled in Japanese. Key! Key!

Lili fought down a freezing wash of panic. She needed to get Lizard out of there before they opened the door, so she did it the most direct way she could: she wrapped her arms around his waist and pulled.

The shock of being grabbed like that—and by a

girl!—made Lizard spin around.

'Lizard, it'll be worse for him if they catch you too.' Lili cupped his face in both hands, looking into his huge, devastated eyes. 'They'll torture *you* to torture him. That will hurt him more than *anything* else, understand? We'll come back for him, all right? I promise!'

They heard a key being shoved into the lock on the other side of the door.

Lili spun Lizard's shoulders around and pushed him up the stairs.

'Quick, you two!' Miss Adelia hissed. She had the top door open and they could see the morning light outside. They scrambled out into a quiet back alley. Miss Adelia slammed the door shut behind them and hurried them along until they finally came out into North Bridge Road.

CHAPTER FOURTEEN

An Infestation of Children

'We can't just leave him there!' Lizard burst out, as Miss Adelia led them into a coffee shop opposite the Tanaka's Emporium shopfront.

'There's nothing we can do right now, Lizard,' said Lili. 'The place is full of gunjin. Don't worry, we'll rescue him.'

Miss Neha was sitting at a table in the window with her coin purse and a cup of coffee in front of her. Lili and Miss Adelia sat down with her. Lizard hovered restlessly, looking out the window towards Tanaka's. Plenty of people were milling around, setting up business or already well into their day. None of them knew anything of what was going on inside that fortress.

Miss Adelia leaned in close to Miss Neha and

began to report the events of the night.

Lili looked at Lizard. He was making her nervous. 'Sit down, Lizard. It will be all right,' she said.

'I'm sorry, I can't just do nothing,' he said, and he swiped Miss Neha's coin purse off the table and ran out the door and across the road. Lili leapt up to follow him, but Miss Adelia grabbed her wrist.

'Let him go, Lili,' she said in a firm but quiet voice. 'We can't risk blowing our cover.'

The three of them stared out the window and watched as Lizard called to a group of boys standing near Tanaka's. Lili wished she was there with him, to keep him out of whatever dumb trouble he was getting himself into.

'Also, Lizard's uncle—' Miss Adelia paused, glancing from Lili to Miss Neha.

'Uncle Archie—he knows Mr Davis,' said Lili, remembering the message he had given Lizard. 'Mr Davis is Maximum Ops too, isn't he? How does Uncle Archie know Mr Davis?'

'Good question. That's another reason we can't get involved,' said Miss Adelia. 'We don't know what mission another Maximum Ops division might be running, and we can't get in their way.'

'You mean Uncle Archie's mission is to be a prisoner there?' said Lili, dismayed.

'I don't know, Lili,' said Miss Adelia. 'But, right now, we can't interfere.'

Across the road, Lizard opened Miss Neha's purse and scattered coins into a growing crowd like a flower girl tossing rose petals at a wedding.

'Well,' said Miss Neha dryly. 'I'm glad I left my twenty dollar bills in my other purse.'

Ah Ling and Ah Keung had been on their way to school, but stopped when they saw Lizard throwing coins.

'Tanaka's has got a new shipment of sweets,' Lizard yelled in Cantonese. 'They're really delicious.' From his pocket, he grabbed the lollies Brylcreem had given him in the shop earlier, and he flung them in a wide arc. Kids jumped and scrambled to get them before they fell into the drain.

'They've got sweets in there,' said Lizard, tossing

the last handful of coins to the growing numbers of kids. 'Lots of sweets, all kinds of sweets.'

In the confusion of the kids grabbing lollies and coins, Lizard reached into the work box of a cobbler working in front of the shop next door and took out a heavy pointed tool. He bashed it against the glass near the door handle of Tanaka's Emporium. The glass smashed, and Lizard reached in and opened the door. 'Come inside. There's lots of sweets!' he yelled as he dropped the tool back in the cobbler's box.

The kids followed him inside. Lizard ran to the large glass jar of lollies on the counter and tossed them all over the shop floor. Giggling kids were everywhere.

The lollies were running out. Lizard looked under the counter and was surprised to see tins of lollies of different kinds on the shelf. He felt sad that Tanaka, a man thoughtful enough to provide sweets for the children of his customers, was involved with the gunjin.

Anyway, he was here to rescue Uncle Archie. If there were any gunjin here, they weren't going to kidnap twenty or thirty shrieking children, especially since some adults, who had noticed what was happening, were coming into the shop. Lizard figured the police would arrive soon too.

'Hey, what are you kids up to?' yelled the man from the shop next door. 'Where's Mr Tanaka?'

Lizard ran to the lift and pressed the button. The usually calm, orderly shop space with its glass-topped counters and cabinets of exquisite silk cloth was filled with children running amok.

Some of the younger kids had even climbed to the top of the cabinets and started pelting lollies at the adults who had come to sort out the commotion. The hooded man had called Georgina and Lizard an infestation of children, but this was what an infestation of children really looked like.

When the grill of the lift finally opened, Lizard stepped in and pressed the basement button.

The riot of over-excited children and cross adults moved out of his view as the lift clanked downwards. It stopped in the basement and Lizard leapt out. But he was too late. The steel cage was empty, and the unlocked chains were lying on the ground. The gunjin had, once again, torn Uncle Archie away from Lizard.

CHAPTER FIFTEEN

Friend or Enemy

Lizard lay on his bunk in his cubicle in Tanjong Pagar Road. He stared at a bloody scratch on the back of his right hand. It must have come from the smashed glass of Tanaka's Emporium door. He picked one end of it, and found a tiny splinter of glass.

Only two nights ago, like all the nights before that for two years, he had lain in his bunk wondering why Uncle Archie had abandoned him. Now he knew that his uncle had been captured by the gunjin and that he hadn't chosen to leave Lizard alone. Lizard was tormented by the thought of what they had done to him and of what they might be doing now.

But why had they captured Uncle Archie? Surely he couldn't have been their prisoner all this time. As far as Lizard knew, his uncle was just an ordinary

British man. But ordinary British men weren't imprisoned by Japanese spies. Should he have seen the clues when he was young? Maybe he should have realised that it wasn't normal for a British man to speak several languages, to live in an isolated stilt house on a remote beach with rural villagers as his nearest neighbours.

Lizard remembered waking one night to hear Uncle Archie speaking in a low voice from his bedroom. He'd got up and found his uncle's bedroom door locked. His curiosity made him sneak outside to go and look in through the window.

The moon had been huge and orange that night, lighting a path across the sea that seemed to end at Uncle Archie's window. The palm fronds high above whispered and rustled in the breeze and the sea shushed rhythmically on the shore as Lizard peered in.

Uncle Archie was sitting at his table, with headphones on. He was bent over a strange box with knobs and wires coming off it. He spoke quietly into a hand-held device, in between smoking a cigarette.

Occasional squeaks and buzzes came from the box, and then a crackly voice. Smoke wreathed the moon-lit room. Lizard had hardly ever seen Uncle Archie smoke. The whole thing had looked mysterious. Lizard didn't understand what was going on, but he knew he wasn't meant to see it. He had crept back to his room.

Now, having watched countless American pictures at the Capitol Theatre, he knew the box was a radio set, for talking to people far away. Who had Uncle Archie been talking to, in such a furtive way?

And all those 'hunting trips' when Uncle Archie had been away for weeks—exactly what had he been hunting?

Lizard wished he had asked more questions. Lili and that silver-haired Miss Adelia were spies. Was it possible that Uncle Archie was a spy too?

'*Wei*, Lizard-ah, got customer for you,' came a voice in Cantonese from outside his cubicle.

'Not now, Ah Mok,' Lizard said, turning to face the wall. 'I mean it.'

'I think you'll want to see this one.' Ah Mok

sounded puzzled and amused at the same time.

'No! Go away.'

'It's like a woman…girl…um, like a Malay woman girl. Asking for you.'

'What?' Lizard didn't know any Malay woman girl who would come asking for him, but his mind was taken off Uncle Archie for a moment.

'Yes, well, she is wearing a Malay hijab. She very loud. Talking English. "Lee-zahrd! Lee-zahrd! You know preetty boy Lee-zahrd?"' said Ah Mok, speaking English in a high-pitched, grouchy way, which gave Lizard a horrible suspicion.

He sat bolt upright, bumping his head on the shelf.

'Ouch!' he said, just as a figure in a hijab and a long shapeless tunic pushed past Ah Mok into the cubicle.

'Oh, thank goodness,' she said, handing Ah Mok a coin and pushing him out. 'Thank you! Goodbye! *Shoo*!'

Ah Mok took the coin, grinned widely at Lizard and left.

'How do the Malay girls stand it?' grumbled the

figure as she ripped the head veil off, revealing red hair tied up in a messy bun.

Lizard stared, dumbfounded, into the wide blue eyes of Georgina Whitford Jones. The eyes were unmistakable, but her face and hands were an odd, brown-yellow colour.

'I told you I could find you.' She reached out with a finger and closed Lizard's jaw for him.

Lizard leapt off his bunk and ran a hand through his hair. He was terribly conscious of the shabbiness and closeness of his space, his shelf with his bowl and chopsticks, and the piles of paper and sacking on his bunk. He hoped it didn't smell too bad (would she notice ginger, garlic, incense, overripe fruit?) and he hoped that she couldn't hear the raucous yelling in the background that was Cantonese people having a pleasant conversation.

Lizard seized the singlet he had carelessly discarded and pulled it over his head. He moved a stack of paper under his bunk. His school clothes and—horrors!—his oldest pair of shorts were hanging on a nail under his shelf. Hoping Georgina somehow hadn't noticed them, he snatched the shorts and shoved them under his bag.

Finally, he turned, giving his singlet a last tug and his hair a last swipe.

Georgina watched all his frenzied manoeuvres with a little smirk.

'Missy Georgina!' said Lizard. 'How did you find me?'

'That was easy. I just came to Chinatown and asked.' She looked all about the narrow, shabby space. Lizard winced and wondered what the chances were that none of the Chinatown boys would hear about it. Zero, he decided.

'Where did you get that outfit?' he said, staring at her in fascination. With her head down and in the dappled lights of a Singapore evening, it would be an effective disguise.

'Our room boy at Raffles. He's so helpful, you just can't imagine.' She smiled smugly, and Lizard wondered what she had threatened Roshan with to make him help her.

'And that colour?' he asked, waggling his fingers

in front of his face.

'Paprika and a little turmeric paste. I've done it before.' She studied the back of her left hand. 'Do you think it suits me?'

Up close, the colour was jarring and unnatural. He'd only ever seen one person anywhere near that colour, and that person had been suffering from malarial jaundice. Also she had missed a bit just in front of her left ear.

'Lovely,' he lied. 'Um...why are you here?' For the life of him, Lizard couldn't even guess at the reason for her visit to his extremely un-Raffles-like cubicle.

Georgina took a step towards him and inspected the shelf over his bed. She smelled of curry powder. It was disturbing.

'Don't you like me being here?' Georgina whispered, turning to look into Lizard's eyes.

He jerked back, bumping his head on the shelf again and then sat down on his bunk.

She laughed and sat down next to him. 'You're so amusing, Dinesh! I want to know how you knew where I was being held by those horrible Japanese men. You didn't have anything to do with my kidnap, did you?'

'No, of course not!' said Lizard, taken aback.

'When I got back to Raffles, I told my father where I'd been held captive. He sent the authorities to Middle Road straight away, and found the place filled with screaming children, but none of those thugs anywhere.'

'Gosh,' said Lizard. 'I guess they knew you'd set the British on them as soon as you could.'

Georgina narrowed her eyes at him. 'Yes, but what about the children? Wouldn't the Japanese have just slipped quietly out the back and got away? Wasn't the door locked?'

'I've no idea,' Lizard lied again. He paused, thinking hard. 'You know how children love lollies. There was a big jar left on the counter. They should be careful of rats too.'

'Hmm,' said Georgina, still staring at him. 'Anyway, how did you find me in the first place?'

Lizard didn't know what to say. Georgina was

clever, and if he said anything, he was likely to say the wrong thing and then Lili would get angry. There was not the slightest doubt in his mind that Lili would find out everything he said to Georgina.

'I can't say,' he said.

'Can't you?' she said, in a steely voice. 'Perhaps, then, you would like to explain why not to my father.'

Lizard leapt off the bunk. 'What? Is he here?'

'No, but he could be,' Georgina said. 'I'm such a naughty daughter, leaving the suite hidden in the dinner trolley pushed by our clever room boy. I'm feeling guilty now and I think I'd better go back and confess to my father *all about you*.'

Lizard gulped. He had not thought about how much trouble he could be in if Georgina told her father about him. He realised that getting rid of the codebook didn't mean his problems with the Whitford Joneses were over at all.

'That's right,' she said, watching his face. 'I haven't once mentioned you to my beloved father. Or that officious girl—what's her name? Something common...oh yes, Lili. It's all very odd and I want to 'know what's going on.'

Lizard kept his mouth shut.

'I listen to my father talking, you know. It's to do with the Japanese and the war, isn't it? He talks to Commander Baxter and I hear what they say. Come on, tell me how you found me after that brute kidnapped me.' She stared expectantly at him.

Thinking about 'that brute' gave Lizard a burst of inspiration. He said, 'I followed you. Yes, that's right. I followed you when that brute grabbed you.'

'Goodness!' she said, impressed. He was enjoying the glow of her blue-eyed admiration, but those eyes suddenly narrowed. 'Wait a minute,' she said. 'They dragged me into a car. A very fast car. Very fast.'

'The truth is, I was sitting at the top of the wall wondering...planning, really, how I was going to rescue you when...' Lizard couldn't think of what to say next. Then, with another burst of inspiration, he continued, 'I saw the car come back up Beach Road from the other direction, more slowly and then I jumped off the wall and followed it and it turned into Middle Road—'

'And then you saw how they had wrapped me in horrible sacking and how they carried me—valiantly struggling—into the shop!' Georgina finished for him. 'Aren't you clever!'

She reached over with her oddly coloured face and pecked him on his cheek. 'That's for you,' she said, as if bestowing a medal.

Lizard was stunned. The kiss wasn't entirely pleasant, with its whiff of curry and condescension. He blushed.

Georgina didn't seem to notice. 'How long have you lived here?' she asked.

'About two years,' he said, relieved at the change of subject.

'You know, the first time I met you I couldn't believe my eyes. At first, I thought you were just another local thief, and I've met plenty of those back in India. But then your face! Not Indian, not Chinese, not English. And then your voice! So British. I couldn't work out where you could possibly belong, but now I see.' She looked around. 'Yes. Now I see.' Her eyes took in the dark blue trilby hanging on the wall, then moved along to the photo of a smiling man in uniform. She leaned in and studied the photo. 'Who's this?'

'Nobody!' he said fiercely, staring at the photo.

'Nobody?' asked Georgina.

Lizard was suddenly panic stricken, as if by denying Uncle Archie, he had somehow lost him all over again. He continued looking at the photo, his eyes tracing the contours of his uncle's face, and comparing this smiling healthy man in the picture with the haggard figure in chains in the emporium basement. 'It's my Uncle Archie,' he said. 'I used to live with him.'

Georgina was quiet for a moment. 'I have three brothers: Frank, Edward and Everard,' she said. 'One by one they were all sent home to England for their education. Sent 'home to England', can you imagine, when we were all born in India! They were all as jolly as anything when they left. When Frank came back to New Delhi last year, I hardly recognised him, he was so pale and stuck up.' Georgina crossed her arms and frowned. 'When Father wanted to send me to

England two years ago I refused. I'd been there once when I was six and all I remember is that it was cold, dreary and grey. Luckily, Mother sided with me and so I got to stay in India.'

Lizard nodded, wondering what all this had to do with him.

'Anyway, Father says we might have to stay in Singapore for a good while. Something to do with the company. Mother and Father are going to look at a company house in a few days, in a place called Tanglin. It's quite near Chinatown so I can sneak out and visit you.' She reached out and patted his hand. 'I knew from the *very first* that we were going to be friends, didn't you?'

Lizard stared at Georgina, horrified. 'But...' he glanced around at his space. 'This is Chinatown. It's lousy! You don't belong here. You have to leave!'

He flinched as Georgina rounded on him. 'Don't tell me I don't belong here! I don't belong anywhere!' Her lip trembled, but her eyes remained defiant. 'We can be friends or we can be enemies. You choose.'

As Lizard looked at Georgina, who was one

moment palm sugar and the next razor blades, all he knew was that if Georgina didn't kill him, then Lili would.

'Friends,' he gulped. 'I choose to be friends.'

CHAPTER SIXTEEN

The Nightingale and the Gamekeeper

'Excellent work, Lili,' said Miss Neha. 'Your copy of the Japanese Navy codebook is a triumph.'

'I don't agree,' said Miss Adelia, sipping her tea. The three of them were back at the Girls' Mission School, having afternoon tea in Miss Neha's study the day after the Tanaka's Emporium incident.

Lili and Miss Neha looked at Miss Adelia, surprised, and, in Lili's case, somewhat dismayed.

Miss Adelia smiled. 'The real triumph,' she said, 'was returning the codebook so that the enemy didn't realise it had been copied.'

'True,' said Miss Neha. 'Who would suspect children of espionage? And a girl, what's more.'

Lili flushed with pleasure at the compliment. Lili had written a complete report for Miss Adelia and

Miss Neha, including Lizard's part in the previous day's events—this was unavoidable, as they had met him already, so she hadn't hidden anything. Lili was relieved that they didn't seem to think he was an enemy spy.

'Well. Neha, I think this outcome more than proves the worth of the S-Stream project, don't you?'

'Guaranteed funding for another year, perhaps?' Miss Neha took a happy sip of her tea.

'Two years, I'd say,' said Miss Adelia, reaching for a chocolate éclair. 'The War Office is very pleased to have the copy of the codebook photographs. Really, these Minox cameras are a wonder!'

'And now the War Office can read the Japanese Naval messages. Sir Wilbur Willoughby is delighted with our work. He has come to Singapore to assess the situation here himself,' said Miss Neha.

Lili had met him only once, but she remembered Sir Wilbur Willoughby, Director of the Asia division of Maximum Operations Enterprise, very well.

'Anyway, enough congratulations,' Miss Neha said, putting down her cup. 'Our work is not over yet.' She took a piece of paper from a file on the desk in front of her. 'Following your excellent decoding work, Lili, we have had the message translated into English by our Maximum Ops Japanese expert.'

Miss Adelia and Miss Neha had been very interested in the envelope that Lizard had found on the floor, with its groups of five-digit numbers scrawled on the back. It was a coded message, perhaps written out to be sent by radio. Lili stayed up late matching the numbers with codes in the photographed pages of the codebook to decipher it, and had ended up with a message in Japanese.

Lili, Miss Adelia and Miss Neha stared at the translated message.

Meet at Raffles 10pm Nov 9
Nightingale has maps and photographs
Nightingale and Mr Nightingale to board boat
midnight Nov 9

'What does it mean?' asked Lili.

'November 9 is in two days' time. And there's

a garden party at the Raffles Hotel Palm Court that night, thrown by the *Malaya Tribune*. They've invited some of the Japanese consulate staff, as well as British top brass.' Miss Adelia said. 'I think the rendezvous will happen there.'

'It would seem likely that one of the Japanese consulate staff is the nightingale. We need to be there to find out who Nightingale is and intercept the maps and photographs,' said Miss Neha.

'But are there two agents? Lili asked 'It says Nightingale and Mr Nightingale in the last line of the message.'

'Good question. I have to admit that we don't know, but we are working on it,' said Miss Neha.

'Could it be a mistake by the message coder?' asked Lili.

'That's a possibility,' said Miss Neha. 'It is unfortunate that we did not get clearer information from the gamekeeper.'

'That's the thing with spies—they won't tell you anything unless they know who you are,' said Miss Adelia.

'Who is the gamekeeper?' asked Lili. 'Uncle Archie said that name.'

Miss Neha and Miss Adelia looked at each other. 'Does she need to know?' asked Miss Neha.

'I rather think she does,' Miss Adelia said. 'The gamekeeper is the code name of one of the top Maximum Ops agents in Asia.'

'But what has the gamekeeper got to do with Uncle Archie?' asked Lili.

'My dear, haven't you realised yet?' asked Miss Adelia. 'Lizard's uncle *is* the gamekeeper.'

'Oh!' exclaimed Lili. 'And Lizard never knew! But Uncle Archie—I mean the gamekeeper—he did not recognise you, did he, Miss Adelia?'

'No, we've never met, but I recognised him, not straight away because of the bruising and... well, let's just say he looked quite different from the photographs we have on file,' said Miss Adelia.

'What did that message mean?' said Lili. '*The gamekeeper says that autumn is coming so get marmalade.*'

'It's not our operation so we don't know the

details, but "autumn" will be the code word for a mission or some sort of intelligence that the gamekeeper was sent to work on,' said Miss Adelia. '"Marmalade" is probably a particular action required from Maximum Ops—a meeting, or perhaps extraction of the agent.'

'Why didn't you tell him you worked for Maximum Ops?' asked Lili.

'Think about it, Lili,' said Miss Adelia. 'He can't tell the gunjin what he doesn't know.'

Lili knew that Miss Adelia meant that he couldn't tell the gunjin what he didn't know under interrogation. And she knew about interrogation methods and how effective they could be.

'Oh, Miss Adelia!' she cried. 'Poor Uncle Archie! We must rescue him!'

It was Miss Neha who answered. 'We have given the gamekeeper's message to Mr Davis. Mr Davis is part of Maximum Ops Asia Division. They will take it from here.'

'But I promised Lizard that we would save his uncle!' said Lili.

'We cannot interfere in another mission,' said Miss Adelia.

'Lili, we are going to need Lizard's help soon. He must be in good condition to be of any use,' said Miss Neha.

Lili look confused.

'What Miss Neha means, Lili, is that Lizard must not be too anxious about his uncle. We are going to need his help in investigating the rendezvous at Raffles Hotel,' Miss Adelia said.

Lili was still puzzled.

'The boy will be no use to us if he is a blubbing mess,' said Miss Neha.

Miss Adelia sighed. 'You must tell Lizard that his uncle is going to be all right and that we have plans to rescue him.'

'Is that true?' Lili asked.

'We know nothing of the gamekeeper's operation. Maybe he will be rescued, maybe not. Perhaps his mission is to remain a prisoner, we don't know,' said Miss Neha. 'But Lizard must not know that. You are an agent for the British Empire, Lili. You must do what is necessary to ensure that Lizard functions effectively in his part of our mission.'

'You mean I must lie to him,' said Lili.

'Pull yourself together, Lili,' Miss Adelia snapped. 'Remember that you've lied to Lizard ever since you've known him, right up until, hmm, let me see...*yesterday*.'

'You performed well yesterday,' said Miss Neha. 'You will be given more missions, but only if we are sure you can handle them. Lying, being undercover— for an agent, these things are necessities. The success of the mission must be put above all else.'

'I've lied to my family and friends for years,' said Miss Adelia. 'My mother lives in Derbyshire. She thinks I teach English at a girls' school. Which I do, but she doesn't know I also teach breaking and entering, weapon handling and codebreaking.'

'Anyway, back to the matter in hand,' said Miss Neha. 'We need to be at the party to find out who the Nightingale is and intercept the handover of the maps and photographs.'

'Lizard has a connection there and he can help us

get in. You tell me, Lili, what is the point of worrying and upsetting Lizard about his uncle?' Miss Adelia stared at Lili.

Lili said nothing.

'Exactly, so you tell him something to stop him worrying,' said Miss Neha. 'All right?'

Lili nodded, reluctantly.

'Now, there is going to be a party at the Raffles tomorrow night. Quite the glittering soiree. And Adelia and Lili, you will both be there.'

Lili felt a twinge of excitement. She was going to a Palm Court party at the Raffles Hotel.

As Lili left Miss Neha's study, she noticed the shoelace on her left shoe was untied. She bent down to tie it, and realised that she could hear Miss Neha and Miss Adelia talking through the not-quite-closed door. They were always so careful when speaking to her and the other S-Stream girls; here was a wonderful opportunity to hear something real and unguarded.

'The boy Lizard—I'm not sure I agree with Sir Wilbur's assessment of him,' said Miss Adelia.

Lili's ears pricked up even further.

'The British are always so suspicious of outsiders,' snorted Miss Neha.

'Not me,' replied Miss Adelia. 'But Sir Wilbur found it odd that the gamekeeper never mentioned the boy to anyone in an official capacity.'

'Because he knew Maximum Ops wouldn't allow him to keep Lizard, nephew or not,' said Miss Neha.

'Do you think we should really let Lizard be there at the Raffles party?' said Miss Adelia.

'No choice. We need him to get Lili in,' said Miss Neha. 'After that, we won't need him anymore.'

'Still,' Miss Adelia heaved a heavy sigh. 'It seems awfully harsh to put a child in detention.'

'I'm sure Sir Wilbur won't put him with the adult detainees,' said Miss Neha.

'Oh, solitary confinement would be so much better, would it?' Miss Adelia snapped.

'It is not my decision, Adelia,' said Miss Neha calmly.

Lili's mouth dropped open. What did they mean by 'detention'? Did they mean a detention centre? A detention centre was just like a prison. It sounded like

Sir Wilbur was suspicious of Lizard after all. Was he planning to lock Lizard up after they had finished using him?

She had no chance to think more about it, as she heard the women getting up and moving to the door. Lili fled silently down the hallway, her untied shoelace flapping as she ran.

CHAPTER SEVENTEEN

The Party at Palm Court

The night of the Raffles Hotel party was humid but clear.

The columns and arches of the Palm Court provided an elegant setting for the party. White flowers on the frangipani trees gave out a sweet, cloying scent.

Candlelit tables glowed under a starry sky, and Chinese lanterns hung between the palm trees. A cleverly lit fountain tossed shimmering water into the night and a string quartet played just beyond it.

Distinguished men in formal suits and smiling ladies in evening gowns chatted in groups, while the wait staff moved among them, carrying trays laden with food and drinks.

The Raffles photographer and his bright lamps

were set up beneath the arches, ready to capture the glamour of the evening.

There were several Japanese consulate staff there. Lili recognised three or four from photographs in her mission file. She wondered which one might be the Nightingale.

'Boy—get me a drink. Chop, chop!' called one of the men in faultless attire, clicking his fingers at Lili.

This was not how Lili had envisioned her night at the Raffles Hotel party—she was dressed as a boy in a white tunic and black trousers, with a short-haired, somewhat shaggy wig on her head, pretending to be a waiter. The guest, she saw as she neared him, was Sebastian Whitford Jones.

She dipped deferentially as she presented him with the tray of Singapore Slings.

Lizard had made Roshan arrange for him and Lili to work at the party. It had taken lies, pleading, threats and bribery to get Roshan to agree to the plan. In the end he had paid two of his waiter friends to tell the maitre'd they were sick ('can't stop vomiting, Sir,' they'd both said, clutching their tummies). Then, just as the maitre'd was about to explode, Roshan had offered the services of two waiters he knew, who he said had experience in fine hotels. Roshan had groaned when the maitre'd had rostered him on to work too.

Lizard worried that Georgina would be at the party and that she would recognise them and give them away, but Lili assured him that their disguises would work if they kept away from her. Things had happened so fast that Lili hadn't had a chance to think much more about what Miss Adelia and Miss Neha had said about Lizard, but it unsettled her. She hoped she had misunderstood them.

But, right now, here they were at the Raffles party, with important work to do.

'Oh, ho, the famous Singapore Sling, invented right here at Raffles Hotel!' said Sebastian Whitford Jones, as he took a pink cocktail from Lili's tray. Lili calmed her nerves by reminding herself that he had never seen her before and couldn't know that she had spied on him and Commander Baxter only a few nights ago.

'Yessir,' she said trying to sound like a boy, but he had already turned his attention to two other guests, strolling towards them. Lili recognised Commander Baxter, and with him was Major-General Arthur Percival, ex-chief of staff to the general officer commanding Malaya. She bet it would be worth her while hanging around to hear what these three had to say.

Major-General Percival stared at the photographer under the arch. The bright glare on his face from the photographer's light washed out his unassuming features, and he blinked and frowned.

He took a drink from the tray Lili offered him, then she moved to a nearby palm tree, next to which was a small table. She stood still, occasionally offering a glass to a passer-by.

'Ah, Major-General Percival, Commander Baxter,' Sebastian Whitford Jones said, as they came up to him. 'Good gracious, both the British Army *and* Royal Navy at Raffles Hotel!' he guffawed. 'Should Singapore be reassured or alarmed?'

'Mr Whitford Jones,' said Major-General Percival.

'Congratulations on your promotion, Major-General,' said Mr Whitford Jones.

'Thank you,' said Major-General Percival. 'Yes, I'm on my way back to London.'

'Malaya will be sad to lose you,' said Commander Baxter.

Lili saw Roshan walking past and stopped him. She was running out of cocktails, so she took some of his full glasses. She thanked him and he continued on his way. She was about to leave Mr Whitford Jones, Commander Baxter and Major-General Percival, who seemed to have nothing interesting to say, to eavesdrop on the Japanese Consulate staff when she heard something that made her stay.

'Bit sorry to leave. The Japanese situation, you know,' Major-General Percival said, eyeing the photographer who turned around just far enough as he adjusted his camera equipment for Lili to notice that he was Japanese. She thought the photographer couldn't possibly hear them over the buzz of the party, but Major-General Percival lowered his voice nevertheless. 'General Dobbie and I are rethinking our strategy for Malaya.'

'We do have our brand new naval base here in Singapore, Major-General,' said Commander Baxter, raising an eyebrow. 'And big guns facing the sea ready for any enemy ships.'

Major-General Percival watched an elegant young couple stroll over to get their photograph taken. The smiling photographer chatted and nodded to them. Percival leaned towards Baxter. 'Down through the Malayan jungle, that's the way they'll come. Not from the sea. It's not impenetrable, that jungle. That's our weakness. Anyway, that photographer—Japanese, isn't he?'

Baxter looked round, squinting. 'Good old Nakajima? Why, yes. Marvellous fellow, for a foreigner. Been here for years.' He guffawed. 'Oh, come now, Major-General, of all the Japanese chaps here, why suspect him of being a spy?'

'Doesn't he have a studio here at Raffles?' the Major-General said.

'Yes. Nakajima is the best photographer on the island. He takes photographs for the *Straits Times* and for the naval base…' Baxter's voice trailed off.

There was a silence.

'Right. I won't keep you,' Percival said at last. 'I'll leave things in your capable hands. I'm leaving early tomorrow.'

Major-General Percival strode past Lili, putting his empty glass on her tray.

'Dash it!' said Baxter. 'Old Percival might be right.'

'Is there a problem?' asked Sebastian Whitford Jones.

'Back soon. I have a telephone call to make. Got to ring a captain about firing a photographer,' said Baxter moodily and he headed to the main building of the hotel.

Lili looked at the photographer. Maybe he was the nightingale, not one of the Japanese consulate staff. That would be clever—she hadn't even considered him.

Lizard was standing still and staring at the photographer. He had almost forgotten that he was holding a tray of canapés and it was tilted at a precarious angle. Mr Nakajima gestured a young couple to a spot in front of his camera with a half bow and a sweep of his right hand, before ducking under the black cloth cover of his camera. There was something familiar yet unpleasant about Mr Nakajima's hand wave and the little bow. Lizard had seen that mocking gesture before.

'Boy,' Mr Whitford Jones called to Lizard.

Lizard startled, nearly dropping his tray of food. He tore his eyes from Mr Nakajima and offered the canapés to Mr Whitford Jones. Then he moved away, and tried not to hurry as he approached Lili.

'*Psst*, Lili!' he said as he sidled up to her.

His eyes were wide with shock and the hand that held the tray shook so much that the canapés were quivering. He clutched her arm with his free hand.

'Ouch!' she said. 'What's wrong? What are you staring at?'

'Shh, keep your voice down.' Lizard jerked his head towards the photographer. 'Him! There! Mr Nakajima—the photographer,' he whispered. 'I think he's the hooded man!'

Lili looked at Mr Nakajima, who was still hidden under his black cloth as he photographed the glamorous young couple. 'Why?' Lili whispered back.

Lizard was puzzled that she didn't look as shocked as he felt. 'I saw him talking to those people and he did that little bow and that thing with his hand'—he showed her the gesture—'and he pretends to be respectful, but he's really just making people do what he wants.'

Lili eyed Mr Nakajima. 'I just heard that he takes photographs for the *Straits Times* and for the navy, which sounds like a perfect cover for a spy.'

'I can't believe it!' said Lizard. 'I had tea and crackers in his studio a few days ago. No wonder he likes to gossip so much!'

'Do you know him?' Lili was surprised.

'Roshan introduced us. He's friends with everyone at Raffles,' said Lizard.

'Now you know why,' said Lili.

'What are we going to do?' said Lizard, feeling shaken and betrayed.

'I must let Miss Adelia know,' Lili said. She put

her tray down on the nearby table and took out a pencil and a piece of paper from her pocket. She scribbled for a few moments while Lizard stood in front of her, trying to look busy while standing still.

'Now,' she said when she was done, 'give me that tray of canapés.'

CHAPTER EIGHTEEN

A Steaming Claypot
of Fish-head Soup

Lili found Roshan in the sweltering kitchen, refilling his tray with drinks. She tapped him on the shoulder. 'Roshan, I need you to—'

'No, no more!' Roshan backed away from her.

'This is the last time I'll ask you to help,' Lili said. 'Please.'

'The last time? You promise?' he said suspiciously.

'Yes,' she said. 'For today, anyway.'

'All right. What do you need?' he said.

Lili whispered some words of instruction. Roshan sighed and gave her a long-suffering look before leaving the kitchen and returning to the party.

He approached Mr Whitford Jones, proffering his tray.

'Hello, room boy. Got you waiting tonight,

have they? You're a busy fellow.' Mr Whitford Jones swapped his empty glass for a full one.

'A lady want to see you, sir,' Roshan said.

'Really? Who?' Mr Whitford Jones glanced around.

Roshan waved at someone, and the crowd parted as if by sorcery. Lili saw Miss Adelia, dressed in a low-cut shimmering gown, drift towards Mr Whitford Jones. Her silver hair sparkled in the light from the Chinese lanterns and cast a shadow over half of her face as she looked up at him.

Lili moved closer, curious to hear what this extraordinary version of Miss Adelia was going to say.

'Well, Mr Sebastian Whitford Jones.' Miss Adelia's voice was low and husky. 'I've been dying to meet you.'

Sebastian Whitford Jones took in her large hazel eyes and fresh, dewy skin and stood up straighter. 'I'm afraid you have the advantage, Miss...'

She took the drink from his hand. 'Why, thank you,' she said. 'Henrietta Dobbie.'

Lili remembered that Miss Adelia had mentioned once that she'd had a childhood pet pig named Henrietta, and she stifled a snort.

'I'm General Dobbie's niece,' Miss Adelia lied with a charming smile. 'Uncle William has told me so much about you!'

'Has he, by Jove?' said Mr Whitford Jones, clearing his throat in a pleased manner, and checking surreptitiously that Mrs Whitford Jones, who was over by the string quartet, wasn't watching him.

'"That Whitford Jones feller,"' said Miss Adelia, adopting a gruff voice. '"Marvellous job he's doing with the company. He's one to watch, you mark my words, Henny-girl."' She broke off with a girlish giggle. Then she dropped her voice so that Mr Whitford Jones had to lean in to hear her next words. He sniffed deeply, no doubt taking in what Miss Adelia called her 'chump-baiting perfume' of jasmine and musk.

'Uncle William told me you were a man who could be relied on. Is that true, Mr Whitford Jones?' Miss Adelia put her hand on his lapel and looked up at him with her eyes wide and trusting.

'Well, *hmmph*. I try to be…' He swallowed visibly. 'Tell me, my dear, what is that mesmerising perfume you are wearing?'

'Oh, do you like it?' Miss Adelia turned her pale, smooth neck to him, the better for him to catch the scent. 'It's…Tabu.'

'Oh? Taboo, is it?' He took out his handkerchief and mopped his brow. 'Jolly warm this evening, isn't it?'

Lili couldn't help feeling some disapproval—the man was married, and Miss Adelia was flirting shamelessly. She decided now was the right time to interrupt.

'Ahem,' she said behind Miss Adelia, who turned and looked into Lili's reproachful eyes.

'Yes, boy?' Miss Adelia asked, unable to stop a tiny wince at Lili's awful wig.

'Canapé, madam?' Lili held out her tray.

'Oh, well.' She arched an elegant eyebrow a fraction to convey to Lili: *Is this interruption necessary? I'm working, you know.*

'The mushroom one is very nice, madam,' said Lili, with a slight inflection in her voice that meant, *Yes it is. There's something you need to know.*

'Well, all right.' Miss Adelia daintily picked up a mushroom canapé, and Lili gave her a red paper napkin that concealed a note.

'For you, sir?' Lili asked, offering the tray to Mr Whitford Jones. 'The chef made very special food tonight, for the very important guests.'

'Really? What have you got, then?' asked Mr Whitford Jones, momentarily diverted.

'This special oyster from Oregon, this caviar from Russia, this anchovy from I don't know where, this...'

While Mr Whitford Jones stood with his hand hovering over the tray, Miss Adelia ate her mushroom canapé and covertly read the note. A small frown flitted across her forehead as she folded the napkin, note still inside it, and patted her lips with it. She turned to look at the photographer, who had just come out from under the black cloth. He smiled and bowed to the young couple as they moved off to re-join the party.

Miss Adelia turned to Lili, crumpled her napkin up and dropped it on the tray.

'There, boy,' she said, a note of dismissal in her voice.

Lili nodded and walked away.

Miss Adelia looked at Mr Whitford Jones, who was holding a canapé in each hand.

'We should have a photograph taken, don't you think, Mr Whitford Jones?' She took his arm. 'Tell me, is that photographer any good?'

'That Japanese feller?' Mr Whitford Jones said, chewing. 'I hear he's the best on the island. Works for the *Straits Times* and the navy, too.'

'Does he, indeed?' Miss Adelia murmured. 'Well come along, Mr Whitford Jones.'

'Oh, do call me Sebastian,' he said as he popped the other canapé in his mouth.

'Well, Sebastian, you must call me Henny. I'm having such a wonderful time.' She gave his arm a cosy squeeze. 'I would love to have a memento of this marvellous evening with you.'

Lili walked away from Miss Adelia, deep in thought. She agreed with Lizard, having observed the photographer, that he was the hooded man from Tanaka's Emporium. The way he had moved with the black camera cover over his head was familiar. His voice was similar too, though his accent was different, but accents, as she well knew, were easily altered.

'Boy!' someone called in a high, clear voice and finger-snapped to get her attention. She looked round to see Georgina Whitford Jones staring at her. The girl's mouth dropped open and her blue eyes bulged. She looked as if she had been slapped in the face with a Malayan giant frog.

'Wh...wh...' Georgina burbled.

Lili cursed her own carelessness. With a sinking heart, she saw Jemima Whitford Jones hurrying towards her daughter.

'Georgina darling, you know you mustn't rush off out like that! You promised—' she began, then she saw her daughter's face. 'Georgina! What's wrong? Oh, I knew it. It's all too much for your delicate constitution.' She flapped her hands, and turned her head. 'Where's your father? Let's get you back to the suite.'

While her mother wittered on, Georgina stared at Lili.

Lili scowled. She put a finger fleetingly to her lips, then stepped away and melted into the crowd, praying that Georgina would have the sense to keep quiet. Things were getting complicated fast. Complications compromised operations. She had to act now.

Across the courtyard, Miss Adelia was standing next to Sebastian Whitford Jones and speaking to the Japanese photographer, no doubt arranging to have their photograph taken.

As Lili approached them, Miss Adelia tripped and her pink drink went splashing down the front of the photographer. Miss Adelia, all charm and apologies, swiftly patted down his pockets. Lili smirked to herself. She would give it a minute, and then go and offer her another Singapore Sling, and find out whether Miss Adelia had found anything interesting on Mr Nakajima. She put on her best waiter's expression, and headed towards Miss Adelia.

Lili was unaware that she herself was being watched. Georgina knew something was going on and she was determined to find out what it was. She wasn't going to let Lili out of her sight. If Lili was here, then Georgina was sure that Lizard would not be far away.

She checked where her mother was, and moved further away from her, hiding behind a group of chatting ladies. Time to see what Lili was up to. She might need help, though.

Unfortunately for Roshan, he chose to walk past Georgina on his way back to the kitchen with a tray of empty glasses at exactly that moment.

'Room boy!' Georgina called.

Roshan stopped as if a steaming claypot of fish-head soup had suddenly appeared at his feet. His face, when he turned to look at Georgina, had the horrified expression of one of those fish heads.

Georgina gestured impatiently. 'Just the person I need. Put down that tray and follow me,' she said.

Lizard lurked behind a palm tree and watched Miss Adelia take a pink drink from Lili's tray. As she pretended to sip it, Miss Adelia's lips moved and Lili leaned in to catch her words. Something glinted in Miss Adelia's hand, and Lizard was sure she slipped the glinting thing to Lili.

A few moments later Lili elbowed Lizard and gestured with the slightest tilt of her head for him to follow her. They both put down their trays on a table and Lizard followed her around the corner to the covered walkway off the Palm Court. No one was around. It was a relief to be out of the noise and lights of the party.

Lizard wondered what was happening. Lili had told him that he was to carry silver trays and walk among the guests eavesdropping for any snippets of information.

Lili stared at Lizard, as if making her mind up about something.

'Miss Adelia will be cross, but time is running out and I need your help,' she said, keeping her voice low. 'You know where Mr Nakajima's studio is, and you've been inside, haven't you?'

'Lots of times,' Lizard said. He grabbed her hand. 'What's that?'

Lili reluctantly opened her hand. 'Miss Adelia took it from Mr Nakajima,' she said.

'Is that the key to Uncle Archie's chains?' asked Lizard, letting go of Lili to touch the key.

'I don't think so,' Lili said. She looked away from him. 'But they'll find him, Lizard.'

Lizard nodded, feeling a little reassured. Maximum Operations Enterprise was a mighty organisation and would save his uncle.

'I need to search the studio,' Lili said.

'Why?' said Lizard. He didn't like the idea of breaking into Mr Nakajima's studio at night, especially now that he knew that Mr Nakajima was the hooded man.

'You cannot tell anyone about this, all right?' said Lili.

Lizard nodded, feeling uneasy. The last person who had said that was Boss Man Beng.

'I think Mr Nakajima is Nightingale,' Lili said.

'Nightingale? What nightingale?' Lizard frowned.

'We used the codebook photographs to decode the numbers on that envelope you found on the floor at Tanaka's Emporium,' she said. She took out a crumpled piece of paper. The message in Japanese was on top, with the English translation below.

Lizard read it out loud. 'Meet at Raffles 10pm Nov 9. Nightingale has maps and photographs. Nightingale and Mr Nightingale to board boat Nov 9 midnight.' He stared at Lili. 'What does it mean?'

'Nightingale is the code name of a spy—Mr Nakajima—and he is going to take maps and photographs onto a boat at midnight tonight,' Lili said. 'But Miss Adelia didn't find any maps or photographs when she patted him down.'

'But there is Nightingale and Mr Nightingale?' Lizard said questioningly.

'Uh—I know,' Lili said.

'How do you say "nightingale" in Japanese?' said Lizard.

'Our Japanese teacher translated it. In Japanese,

"nightingale" is "*uguisu*" and "Mr Nightingale" is "*Uguisu-san*".' I don't know if it's the exact species of nightingale—'

'What did you say?' exclaimed Lizard. 'What's the word for nightingale?'

'*Uguisu*,' said Lili.

Lizard stared at her, his heart hammering.

'I know where there is an *uguisu*,' Lizard said. 'It's an actual bird in a cage, not a person. It's in Mr Nakajima's studio.'

'Oh!' said Lili. '"*Uguisu*" is a real bird, but "*Uguisu-san*" is a man.'

Lizard nodded, feeling sick as he realised who uguisu-san must be. 'Who was the last man you saw in a cage?'

Lili's eyes widened. 'Not...'

'Yes,' said Lizard. 'Uncle Archie.'

CHAPTER NINETEEN

A Silent Scream

'Uncle Archie might be in the studio! And the maps and photographs must be there too,' said Lili. 'Can you show me the way?'

'I certainly can,' said Lizard.

They crept along the sides of the covered walkways and arcades, until they came to the Bras Basah wing, in front of the photographic studio of Mr Nakajima.

'You keep a look out, while I open the door,' Lili whispered to Lizard, and she took her lock-picking set from her pocket.

'What about the key Miss Adelia gave you?' asked Lizard.

'That key is for a padlock, not a door,' she said as she inserted a wire tool and twisted it.

'Someone's coming!' Lizard heard voices from further up the passage. 'Hurry up.'

'It won't turn,' said Lili, sweat beading on her forehead.

Now they could both hear a loud nasal voice. '...and then we heard that duffer Barmy Partridge shout, "Run! It's a ruddy great tiger!" They got jammed in the doorway, of course. Well, we couldn't resist, so we hurled the tiger skin right at them. You should have heard them shriek!'

A high-pitched giggle followed. 'Oh, Cyril! I do wish I'd been there. You're ever so funny.'

The couple came around the corner: a blonde lady clutching a tall, thin man's arm looked up adoringly at him.

'Stop them coming!' hissed Lili, struggling with the lock.

Lizard stumbled towards them. 'No go here, sir, madam,' he said, breathless with nerves.

The couple stopped abruptly. The man frowned down his nose at Lizard. 'Why ever not?' he said.

'Uhh...not very good here, got big, big problem.'

Lizard racked his brains for something else to say. He looked at the lady, and the look on her face gave him inspiration.

'Very smelly here. Got bad plumbing problem.'

'*Eew!*' The lady drew back.

'Are you sure, young feller-me-lad?' the man asked, craning round Lizard and sniffing deeply. 'I can't smell anything.'

Lizard glanced back and saw Lili now standing, arms folded, head turned to look in the opposite direction.

'Yah, is brown, smelly stuff. You come nearer you can smell.' He waved his hand in front of his face. He considered waving his hand behind his bottom, but instead he leaned conspiratorially towards the man. 'We waiting for the plumber. Is not nice for lady to see.'

'Oh, come, Cyril. Let's go the other way.' The lady backed up, pulling on the man's arm.

'Well, all right, Lavinia, just as you say,' said the man. 'Cheerio, then. Thanks for the heads up.'

'Have a good evening, sir, madam,' said Lizard,

relieved. He watched them walk back to the corner.

Just as Lizard was about to join Lili, Cyril turned to look hard at him. 'Wait a minute, old boy!' he called out.

Lizard froze. He watched him speak to the lady, who waited as Cyril walked back to Lizard and loomed over him.

Lizard gulped as he got a good view up Cyril's flared nostrils. He tensed, ready to run.

'I just wanted to say thanks.' Cyril winked at Lizard. He pressed a coin into his hand, and then he strode off into the evening with the pretty lady.

Lizard looked at the silver coin. Twenty cents—more than he got for writing a letter. He pocketed it and went back to Lili.

'Got it,' she said, as she swung the door open. 'Good work.'

'I learn from the best.' Lizard grinned.

They stepped inside the studio and Lili locked the door behind them.

Georgina ignored the laughing English couple as she

walked past them, and Roshan kept his eyes down as he reluctantly followed her. She peeked round the corner and saw Lili and Lizard slip inside the Raffles photographic studio.

'Don't dawdle,' she said to Roshan as she hurried to the door. She turned the handle and tutted in annoyance. 'Locked.' She took a hairpin out of her hair and bent down to fiddle in the lock. 'I'm sure I can do it this time.'

Roshan watched her for a while. 'I could go get the key,' he offered.

'What?' Georgina said.

'The master key. For all the shops and businesses. It's in Mr Arathoon's office. Next to the kitchen. By the—'

'All right, all right, I don't need an essay.' Georgina flapped her hand. 'Hurry up and get it.'

Roshan scurried off into the night.

Inside the studio, Lili switched on the light.

'Isn't that a bad idea?' asked Lizard, blinking in the sudden glare. He was disappointed to see that

Uncle Archie was obviously not in the room.

'We need light to see, and it's easier to explain if we're caught than sneaking around with a torch,' said Lili.

The studio looked just as Lizard remembered it, only everything had an air of menace about it now that he knew Mr Nakajima was the hooded man. There was a table and a chair to his left. Past them, by the far wall, were the backdrop screens and a lot of props. On his right was the darkroom door and the wall with photographs on display.

At the back of the room was the table with the paper screen on it. Was the *uguisu* still behind it? Lizard hurried to the table and moved the screen aside. Yes! Here was the bird, looking inquisitively at him through the bars of its cage.

'Is that the nightingale?' said Lili, coming up next to him.

'The *uguisu*,' Lizard corrected. 'It's not much to look at, but it sings very well. Although it doesn't sing much. No wonder. I wouldn't like to be locked up like that.'

'You'll never be locked up like that,' said Lili, staring at Lizard.

'Okay,' said Lizard, slightly confused. 'Where would you hide maps and photographs?'

'Uh—here,' Lili said, pointing to the bottom of the cage. 'There's usually a part you can pull out for cleaning.'

Lizard pulled a small handle, and the bottom of the cage slid out. The bird fluttered slightly on its perch, but didn't seem disturbed. Lizard peered under the tray. 'There's quite a lot of space between the bottom of the tray and the bottom of the cage. But it's empty.'

'Are you sure?' Lili put a hand inside the space and searched. 'You're right. But the meeting is not until 10pm. Maybe they'll put the maps and photographs in there just before they leave for the boat.'

'That means they'll be back pretty soon,' Lizard said in alarm.

'So we better find the papers before they come.' Lili slid the tray back in, put the screen back and stood up.

'Well, my guess is if there are secrets, they'll be in there,' Lizard said, gesturing at the darkroom door. 'That's where Mr Nakajima develops his film for his photographs.'

Lili headed towards the darkroom door but stopped short. She looked at the photographs on the wall next to the door.

'What a nerve!' she fumed.

'Sorry?' said Lizard, raising his eyebrows.

'Look at this! Army officers, the harbour, even the Naval Base!' Lili gestured at the photographs. 'Anyone would know straight away a spy took them!'

Lizard stared at them. 'Yes,' he said, rubbing the back of his neck, which felt rather warm. 'Straight away, sure. Gosh. What a cheek. Yes.'

Lili tried the handle. 'I'll never go anywhere without this again,' she said, holding up her lock-picking tool.

'Do you think I should cause a real plumbing problem in case someone comes by?' asked Lizard.

'Yuck!' said Lili, without stopping her lock-picking efforts.

'I don't mean that,' protested Lizard. 'I mean pour water on the floor or something.'

'I think it's better if we try to get in and out without anyone knowing we were here. All right, got it.' She twisted the handle and opened the door.

Lizard turned the light on and the room filled with a red glow. Uncle Archie wasn't here either.

Lili turned the light off in the studio before joining Lizard in the darkroom.

'This red light is for developing film. There should be another switch...that's it,' she said, as Lizard turned it on. The space was very neat.

'Smells bad in here.' Lili wrinkled her nose. 'Like vinegar and rotten eggs.'

'It's the chemicals,' Lizard said, pointing to the row of glass bottles on a shelf above a long metal sink to their left. A wooden bench with a curtain beneath it ran along the back wall.

Lili turned to a cupboard on her right and opened its doors. There were some clothes on hangers on the left side and shelves with photographic equipment on the right. She took down a box of metal clips. A few fell out and she quickly picked them up.

'What are these for?' she asked Lizard as she dropped the clips back in the box.

'Hanging up the photographs to dry,' he replied. 'Don't bother with that cupboard. It's too obvious. There won't be anything worth finding in there.'

'Max Ops training: search methodically,' said Lili, putting the box of clips back in the cupboard.

'Real life training: not secret enough,' said Lizard. 'Also, time running out.'

He went to the bench, knelt down and flipped the curtain up. There was a large cardboard box under it. Lizard reached in and pulled it out. It was surprisingly light. In fact it was empty.

'Well lookee here, missy,' said Lizard, pointing to a padlocked trapdoor set into the floor.

'Don't call me missy,' Lili said, crouching down next to Lizard. She took out the key that Miss Adelia had given her. 'I hope this key fits because that padlock looks very hard to pick.'

'Wait!' Lizard whispered in alarm. 'Did you hear something?'

They kept still, hardly daring to breathe. After a minute, Lili whispered, 'Nothing to hear now. What was it?'

'I heard a scrape,' Lizard whispered back.

'Probably from outside, cleaning staff maybe.' She looked at the space under the bench, and at the box. 'Fold up the box so there will be room for us in case we need to hide behind the curtain.'

Lizard did as she said and stashed the box flat against the wall under the bench, while Lili unlocked the padlock and opened the trapdoor. Lizard held his breath as she lifted the lid—would Uncle Archie be there?

'Look!' Lili whispered excitedly. Lizard peered into the space and was disappointed to see that it wasn't big enough to hold a man. But there was a radio and a set of headphones. Next to them was a large brown envelope. Lili pulled the envelope out and handed it to Lizard.

'Take a quick look,' she said, while she pulled out her spy camera. She took a photograph of the radio, then put the camera away again.

'What's there?' she said, as Lizard pulled a few pages out of the envelope. There were photographs of docks, naval ships and aeroplanes and maps of the Malay Peninsula, with red crosses marked on them. There were also several sheets of numbers and Japanese script.

'Maps,' Lizard said.

'Invasion plans,' Lili said. 'All in code! I can't wait to smash their stupid code into a thousand pieces.'

Lizard pointed to a map that showed Raffles Hotel circled in red, with some Japanese writing next to it.

'That bit's not coded. What does it say?' asked Lizard.

'"Inform pilots to avoid this target!"' Lili translated, scowling. 'They must have other plans for Raffles.' She took the envelope from Lizard. 'Let's go. We're done.'

'Are you going to take photographs of all this?' asked Lizard.

'No time. We must get out of here. We're taking it all with us.' She turned her back on Lizard, folded the envelope in half and tucked it inside the front of her trousers. Lizard tried to be polite and not look.

They moved out from under the bench. Lili shut the trapdoor and locked the padlock.

Just then, the front door rattled and two male voices spoke in Japanese as they entered the studio. One of them sounded annoyed.

Lili and Lizard stared at each other, horrified. 'Quick, get back under here!' Lili hissed, gesturing to the bench. Lili leapt to switch the light off and felt her way in the darkness to the bench, where she ducked under the curtain and squeezed in next to Lizard.

Just as the curtain drifted back down again, the door opened and the room filled with light. Lili and Lizard were squashed up against each other, their knees tight against their chests, shoulders scrunched in. Lili couldn't see Lizard's face, but she could hear him breathing into her ear. Her left palm was pressed on the floor with her little finger touching the curtain. In fact, she wasn't certain that a tiny part of it wasn't poking out but she was too scared to move it.

The men were moving around the room. Lizard recognised the voices of Mr Nakajima and Nobu.

Through the curtain, Lili saw the shadow of Mr Nakajima approaching the bench. He was complaining about how Miss Adelia's Singapore Sling had spilt on his camera. They heard him put the camera on the bench.

Then the cupboard door creaked open and clothes hangers moved on the metal rail. Mr Nakajima must be changing his stained shirt, thought Lili. The grumbling continued, mixed with the sound of clothes being thrown into the metal sink.

After a year of Japanese lessons at school, Lili could understand much of what the men were saying: mostly unflattering comments about the British partygoers and how undisciplined they were.

'It makes me sick to bow and smile to these Westerners who think they are so superior to us. When we sweep in right under their noses and take over'—here Lili listened hard—'then we will be the ones laughing.'

Mr Nakajima put the clothes he had just taken

out of the cupboard onto the bench. Lili and Lizard both held their breath.

Suddenly, Lili felt an enormous pain in her little finger. Mr Nakajima had stepped on it. His shoe ground down on her finger, and her mouth stretched open in a silent, agonised scream. Then, to her immense relief, Mr Nakajima moved away, complaining that he would have to wear stained socks as he didn't have another pair in the cupboard.

'*Hai*,' Mr Nakajima said. 'Enough for one night. Those British fools know nothing of the Emperor's intentions. That officer Percival—ha! No idea that our plans to invade Malaya are so advanced. With officers like that, a bunch of pink-faced snow monkeys could take Singapore.'

Lili and Lizard hardly dared to hope that Mr Nakajima and Nobu were leaving now, and that they might get away without being discovered.

'I'll get one of the room boys to have my clothes laundered tomorrow,' Mr Nakajima said. He shut the cupboard door, then walked towards the door. 'Don't forget to turn out the light.'

'*Hai!*' said Nobu as he followed him. But then he stopped. To her horror, Lili heard him say, '*Matte kudasai.*' Wait. '*Nan desu ka?*' What is that?

Her heart was thumping too fast to do anything. She knew, just knew, that she had left something on the floor...

'*Kurippu?*' Mr Nakajima's slow voice confirmed her awful suspicion. *Kurippu*. Clip. One of the clips she had dropped must still be on the floor. Mr Nakajima was not a man who would carelessly leave a clip on the floor like that. She knew it, and Nobu knew it too.

There was silence. Then one set of footsteps moved towards the bench. Lili glanced at Lizard before the curtain was yanked back and they both looked straight into Mr Nakajima's furious face.

CHAPTER TWENTY

The Key to the Trapdoor

Mr Nakajima moved aside, and Nobu's menacing features filled the space. He reached in, dragged Lizard and Lili out from under the bench and dumped them on the floor.

'Lizard-san!' Mr Nakajima said, looking genuinely puzzled. 'What? Why are you here?'

'I...' said Lizard.

Mr Nakajima's eyes darted to the space where Lili and Lizard had been hiding. Fortunately, Lili had re-locked the padlock.

'Uh, sorry, sir,' said Lili, looking ashamed.

'We just wanted see what your darkroom was like,' said Lizard with a gulp. 'I've never been in here before.'

'Really,' said Mr Nakajima, looking unimpressed.

'Why didn't you ask, instead of sneaking around like rats in the night?'

'Someone dared us to break in,' said Lizard.

'I don't believe you,' said Mr Nakajima.

Lili flung herself at Mr Nakajima. 'Oh, please! Please!' she sobbed. 'We were only exploring!' She grabbed at his shirt, and he stepped back with a look of disgust.

Mr Nakajima raised his hand to hit her, and Lizard leapt towards him and pushed his arm away. Mr Nakajima, caught unaware, fell back against the sink. He straightened up, brushed himself down and slapped Lili hard across the face. Her head jerked sideways, and her wig slipped slightly.

'Ow!' she yelled and burst into tears, as loudly as she could.

Nobu reached out and snatched off her wig.

Lizard swung a wild punch at Mr Nakajima, but Nobu grabbed his arm out of the air; it was a mere toothpick in Nobu's meaty paw. Nobu shoved him, and Lizard fell, scraping his face against the corner of the sink.

In the kerfuffle, Lili slipped the padlock key out of her pocket and threw it into the sink. It clunked as it hit the bottom.

'Stop that noise or I will hit you again!' Mr Nakajima said.

Lili stopped howling, and just stood, sobbing. All the time, she was trying to work out how to escape.

'Out,' Mr Nakajima said to Nobu.

Nobu grabbed Lizard and Lili by the scruffs of their necks and hustled them into the main studio. Lizard's right cheek was bleeding from its scrape on the corner of the sink, and Lili's face throbbed from Mr Nakajima's slap.

Lili figured Mr Nakajima wanted them out of the room where he kept all the incriminating evidence. He stood, arms folded, and watched them leave his darkroom. As he turned to follow them, his eye fell on the padlocked trapdoor.

He started and reached into his jacket pocket, then glanced at the sink where he had thrown his stained clothes. With a worried exclamation he hurried to the sink and searched through the clothes.

Lili, the back of her neck grasped in Nobu's huge left hand, saw the relief on Mr Nakajima's face when he found the key. She willed him not to unlock it. *Don't open the trapdoor. We're just stupid children. That padlock's never been unlocked. You've had that key all the time.*

Mr Nakajima stared at the padlock for an agonisingly long moment, then pocketed the key. He came out of the darkroom and shut the door.

'Nobu, tie them up,' he said.

Nobu looked around. The various screens, chairs, plants, hats and other photographic props were neatly arranged on one side of the studio. He spotted some silk scarves and reached out for them, letting Lizard go in order to do so. 'Don't move or the girl will get hurt,' he said.

Lili dangled in Nobu's grip like a mouse-deer in a tiger's jaws, and Lizard stood very still.

Nobu wrapped a scarf around Lili's wrists.

She tensed her forearms as he knotted the scarf and pushed her to the floor.

'Stay there,' he rumbled. Then he patted Lizard

down, pushed him onto the chair and tied his arms behind the back of it. Lizard wondered how something as delicate as silk could make such a strong bond.

'Now, explain yourself,' Mr Nakajima said, perching on the edge of the table next to Lizard.

Lizard gulped. The tea-drinking, cracker-crunching, harmless photographer of Lizard's fond acquaintance was now his threatening interrogator. He tried to think of a lie that would get him out of this, but the lies wouldn't come. All he could think of was how the gunjin were so cruel in China, and of Uncle Archie's thin, bruised face.

'Lizard-san,' said Mr Nakajima. 'In front of you is Mount Fuji.' He gestured without looking at a screen behind him. The screen showed the cone-shaped mountain topped with snow and framed by pink cherry blossoms. 'So peaceful, yes? The last eruption was two hundred years ago: villages destroyed, Tokyo buried in ash. Volcanoes are best kept peaceful, Lizard-san. So'—he leaned in close to Lizard's face—'answer my question.'

Still Lizard didn't—couldn't—say anything. He forced himself not to look at Lili, who was sitting on the floor a few metres away.

Mr Nakajima shook his head. '*Tanto*,' he said, looking at Nobu. Nobu reached under his jacket in the region of his waist and took out some sort of scabbard. From this, he pulled a sharp, shiny knife.

Icy needles of terror pricked the back of Lizard's neck.

Nobu moved behind Lizard, grabbed him by his hair and pressed the flat of the blade to his right cheek. The pressure re-opened the cut on his face, and it started bleeding again.

'You've already injured yourself. The first layer of skin is the epidermis,' said Mr Nakajima.

Lizard jerked his head back.

'I had anatomy lessons in the Navy, you know,' said Mr Nakajima. 'Now talk, Lizard-san.'

'What do you want to know?' Lizard managed to say, his voice cracking with fear.

'Why are you here?' Mr Nakajima's voice was deceptively calm.

Frightened though he was, one thought forced its way to the front of Lizard's brain. *Say nothing about Lili.*

'I'm looking for Uncle Archie,' he blurted out. Out of the corner of his eye, he saw Lili shake her head hard.

Mr Nakajima raised his eyebrows. He gestured at Nobu, who let go of Lizard's hair and stepped back.

'Uncle Archie,' Mr Nakajima said slowly. 'Our British prisoner. The one in Tanaka's.'

Lizard dropped his gaze to the floor. He realised he had made a big mistake—Uncle Archie was the spy who Mr Nakajima had captured and interrogated. *And Lizard had just told him the spy was his uncle.*

He felt the blood rush to his face. Mr Nakajima wasn't trying to hide the fact that he was the hooded man. This was bad.

Mr Nakajima stood up, moved towards Lizard and bent down to stare into his eyes.

'Is that Englishman your *uncle*?' He drew the

words out with a soft, measured relish that made Lizard shudder with dread.

'Now it all makes sense. I couldn't understand why you were so reluctant to leave Tanaka's basement, but now I see,' Mr Nakajima said, standing up. 'We have had him for quite some time. Yet no matter how we try to persuade him, he refuses to tell us what we need to know. But now'—he reached out his hand and, with the back of one finger, stroked Lizard's left cheek lightly—'I think he will sing like the *uguisu* in springtime.'

Lizard recoiled, his lip curling with disgust.

'But first, I want you to tell me all about him. Start with his full name.'

Mr Nakajima waited.

Lizard pressed his lips together and looked away.

Mr Nakajima waved at Nobu who grabbed Lizard's hair again, pulling his head back. The knife blade pressed further into Lizard's cheek. 'The second layer is called the dermis,' Mr Nakajima said. 'This layer is rich in blood vessels.'

Lizard's breath came in short panting gasps now,

and he was light-headed with terror. He tried to twist away but Nobu's grip was too tight. 'Tell me about Uncle Archie,' said Mr Nakajima softly. 'Nobu will stop, when you talk.'

Nobu let go and Lizard's head jerked forward. A drop of blood fell onto his tunic. Both Lizard and Mr Nakajima looked at it, the red stark against the white.

Lizard was suddenly sure that he would be killed whether he talked or not. If he didn't say any more, he couldn't make things worse for Uncle Archie, and maybe Lili could get away. He made a decision—he might die, but he wouldn't talk.

Once he'd decided that, his breathing slowed and his brain cleared. He gritted his teeth, lifted his eyes and stared at Mr Nakajima. Lizard shook his head, barely perceptibly, just once.

The corners of Mr Nakajima's mouth lifted a fraction, as if in grudging admiration. '*Yuuki, ne?*' he said, glancing at Nobu.

Lili knew *yuuki* meant 'courage' and was one of the samurai virtues. However, she also knew Mr

Nakajima was not going to stop interrogating Lizard.

Mr Nakajima sighed as if regretting the things he was going to do next.

Lili's heart squeezed with fear for Lizard. She bit at the silk to try to loosen the knot, but it was too tight. Lizard was already bleeding and she couldn't do anything. Deep breath. Calm, she told herself. She couldn't untie the silk but there was always another way. Just work it out. She moved herself to a kneeling position and got ready.

'Underneath the dermis is the fat layer, then the buccinator muscle. And after this we are in the mouth itself,' said Mr Nakajima. He clicked his fingers and said to Nobu, 'Do it.'

Nobu stepped forward once more, grabbed Lizard's hair and raised his knife.

'No!' Lizard kicked out hard. His foot caught Mr Nakajima in the stomach, doubling him over with a grunt.

Mr Nakajima straightened up. He took a deep breath and a large step back. 'Good, Lizard,' he said. 'You show a samurai spirit. You strike when it is right to strike. It is a pity that you are not Japanese. You are a waste of great potential.'

Behind Mr Nakajima, the screen of Mount Fuji started to teeter. Lizard watched wide-eyed as it finally tipped and fell forward, crashing onto Mr Nakajima, whose head and torso erupted through the paper volcano.

At the same time Lili launched herself off the floor.

'Nobu!' she yelled, and as Nobu turned towards her she headbutted him full in the face. His nose flattened with a sickening crunch and burst with a shower of blood. He dropped the knife, and reeled back with an agonised moan.

Mr Nakajima was trapped in a mess of broken paper and wooden frame. His face was purple with shocked outrage. He twisted around, and both he and Lizard looked up and saw Georgina Whitford Jones raise a large turquoise crackle-glazed vase high with both hands.

'No!' Mr Nakajima shouted as Georgina brought the vase down with unstoppable force onto his head, where it shattered loudly into a thousand pieces. The man thudded to the floor like a falling durian, breaking the frame of the screen.

Georgina dusted her hands and tossed her red hair over her shoulder. 'I'd rather not have Lizard damaged any more, thank you very much,' she said.

Lizard stared at her. 'How?' he gasped. 'How can you be here?'

'I followed you,' said Georgina. 'Oh! Look at your face!'

Lili sat, stunned, on the floor.

Nobu's hands cupped his nose. Blood oozed between his fingers, and his maddened, watering eyes glared at her. 'I break you!' he roared as he straightened up. He stretched out his bloodied hands, grasping at Lili. Blood continued to splatter from his nose onto his shirt and onto the floor as he moved towards her with the relentless menace of red-hot lava.

Lili scrambled backwards until she hit the wall.

One more step and he would seize her with those huge, blood-dripping hands. But as he surged forward, he suddenly flipped up and backwards and his boots flicked past Lili's astonished eyes. He fell, cracking his head on the back of Lizard's chair as he thumped to the ground.

Nobu lay still, but several small red things rolled towards Lili. She reached out and picked them up. 'Saga seeds?' she said, flabbergasted. She looked up to see Roshan bounce out from behind a screen and beam at Lizard.

'I told you, my friend!' Roshan exclaimed. 'I told you the seeds were lucky!' He gestured down, and Lili looked round and saw more of the hard smooth seeds scattered around the unconscious Nobu.

'What did you do?' Lili asked Roshan.

'I carry my lucky seeds all the time. I could see that big fellow was going to get you so I rolled them out for him to stand on,' Roshan said. 'Very slippery things.'

Just then, the door crashed open and Miss Adelia burst in. Her mouth dropped open in a most unladylike manner at the sight in front of her. She picked up the knife that Nobu had dropped and cut Lili's bonds with it. 'What happened here?' she asked, as Lili stood up.

Georgina stepped over the unconscious Mr Nakajima and bent down to Lizard. He leaned back as she peered at his face.

'Ow,' he winced.

Lili took the knife from Miss Adelia and limped over to Lizard. She elbowed Georgina aside and gently lifted Lizard's chin.

'Of all the nerve!' Georgina started, hands on her hips, but Lili ignored her.

Lili studied Lizard's cheek. Then she gently held his chin and angled his face to the light. He winced again but didn't move. It had stopped bleeding.

Lili turned to Georgina, handed her the knife and said, 'Cut him loose.'

It didn't take long for Georgina to cut through the silk. Lizard shook and rubbed his arms, looking relieved to be alive.

Lili turned back to Miss Adelia, who had just finished checking the men lying on the floor.

'Both breathing,' Miss Adelia said. 'Quick report, please, Lili.'

Lili drew Miss Adelia across to the darkroom and went inside. In a low voice, she told her everything that had happened.

'And they never knew you had the maps and photographs hidden away?' asked Miss Adelia.

'No!' Lili's voice was an indignant squeak. 'They didn't even look in my direction, once I was tied up. All their attention was on Lizard.'

'Of course, you're just a girl.' Miss Adelia gave a brief smile, as she approached the long sink. 'They'd never suspect a girl of espionage. That's why we're going to set this place on fire.'

'What?' Lili said, surprised. 'Why?'

'They'll think the maps and photographs burnt up, and they won't know we've got them.' Miss Adelia studied the bottles of chemicals on the shelf over the sink. She picked out two bottles. 'Highly flammable,' she said, reading the label of one of them. 'Just the ticket. Stand back.' She raised the bottles high over her head and smashed them on the floor, right onto the trapdoor.

As she and Lili left the darkroom, Miss Adelia

opened her small silver handbag and took out a box of matches.

'Will that be enough chemicals?' asked Lili.

'My word, yes,' said Miss Adelia. 'Mustn't over egg the pudding. Can't burn all of Raffles, can we.'

In the studio, Georgina was pulling Lizard to his feet.

'Actually, it might be an improvement,' Georgina was saying to Lizard as she looked at the cut on his face. 'Adds a touch of ruggedness.'

Miss Adelia hustled Lili into the studio. She turned, surreptitiously lit a match, threw it into the darkroom and shut the door.

'Time to go, everybody,' she said, and she clapped her hands. 'Chop, chop. And drag those men outside. Goodness, is that smoke I can smell?'

'Who is that lady?' asked Georgina as she stared at Miss Adelia.

Lili and Lizard, who were hauling Mr Nakajima towards the door, paused and looked at each other. 'I don't know,' they said simultaneously.

Smoke was starting to flow out through the

keyhole of the darkroom door now and they could hear the crackle of flames on the other side of the door.

'Young man,' Miss Adelia said to Roshan. 'Do please help me pull this large fellow outside.'

Surprisingly quickly, the five of them had Mr Nakajima and Nobu out on the grass outside the studio.

'I nearly forgot!' said Lizard and, before Lili could stop him, he dashed back inside. A few moments later, a bird flew out, followed by puffs of smoke and then a coughing Lizard.

'The *uguisu*,' Lizard explained. 'It doesn't sing much, but at least it's free now.'

From outside, they could see smoke billowing into the studio, and a few flames licking under the darkroom door.

'You all right, man?' Roshan said to Lizard, clapping him on the shoulder.

'Yes—' Lizard started, but Roshan didn't wait to hear anymore. He melted away into the darkness.

'Thank you for your help,' Miss Adelia said to

Georgina. 'You might wish to leave rather smartly now. I expect a large crowd will soon gather, which will probably include your parents. Depends, of course, on how much explaining you wish to do.'

'Oh, gosh. I'll see you later,' Georgina said to Lizard. 'After all, now that I know where you live, I can easily visit you again.' She took off towards the Palm Court at a ladylike trot.

Mr Nakajima and Nobu started to stir and moan.

'How,' enquired Lili, turning to Lizard, 'does she know where you live?'

Luckily for Lizard, Lili was distracted when Miss Adelia opened her handbag and took out a photograph. It was of the Singapore Naval Base and it had some words in Japanese written on it. Miss Adelia put it on Mr Nakajima's chest.

'Evidence of espionage. I expect Commander Baxter will arrest Mr Nakajima and his large friend here when he sees this photograph,' said Miss Adelia. She pointed across the garden. 'Quick, go wait there and mix with the crowd as they come in.'

Lili and Lizard hurried to the covered walkway

opposite the studio.

'Help!' Miss Adelia screamed. 'Fire! Fire!' Then, she too, hurried over to join Lizard and Lili.

As the smoke poured out of the studio, people came running into the grassy courtyard. Flames licked out the door. Mr Arathoon shouted for a hose.

When Commander Baxter arrived, Miss Adelia went up to him. 'Oh, commander, those poor Japanese men ran out of the fire and collapsed!' She grabbed his arm and pulled him towards Mr Nakajima and Nobu, who were still lying on the grass moaning. Miss Adelia picked up the photograph from Mr Nakajima's chest.

'What's this?' she said, and put it in the commander's hand. As he frowned at it suspiciously, she backed away.

Lili grinned. 'It's time to go,' she said and they followed Miss Adelia out of the busy courtyard and into a quiet area under some stairs.

'Show me what you found, Lili,' Miss Adelia said.

Lili pulled out the envelope. As she pulled the papers out of the envelope, something fell out of it.

Lizard picked up two rectangles of cardboard.

'They're boarding tickets,' said Miss Adelia, reading the print. 'For the cargo ship, *Senko Maru*, departing the harbour midnight tonight, from the Main Wharf. Let's go.'

Lili and Lizard followed Miss Adelia as she ran out of Raffles Hotel into Bras Basah Road, where a black car was parked.

'Singapore Harbour, Main Wharf. Hurry,' Miss Adelia said to the driver as they got in.

The driver looked at Lizard in the rear-view mirror and raised an eyebrow.

'This is Lizard,' Miss Adelia said to the man. 'Lizard, this is Mr Bee.'

Lili turned to Miss Adelia. 'We've already recovered the maps and photographs, and caught the spies. Why do we need to go to the ship?'

'Maximum Ops Asia Division require extraction of the gamekeeper. Remember the message we decoded? What was the last line?'

Lili frowned in concentration. '*Nightingale and Mr Nightingale to board boat midnight Nov 9.*'

'*Uguisu-san*,' said Lizard. 'Uncle Archie will be on that ship!'

CHAPTER TWENTY-ONE

The Harbour

As the black car tore down Connaught Drive along the waterfront, Lizard glanced up at the Victoria Memorial Hall clock tower. Five minutes to midnight. He was bewildered by everything that was happening. He only understood one thing: they were going to rescue Uncle Archie before he sailed away—but only if they made it in time.

The car drew up at the harbour entrance. Lili, Lizard, Miss Adelia and Mr Bee got out and ran along the harbourfront dodging people. The harbour was busy even as midnight approached.

'There!' Lizard yelled, and pointed at a passenger-cargo ship docked just ahead. They stopped, panting for breath. *Senko Maru* was painted on the ship's bow in English and with Japanese characters underneath.

It was medium sized, for a cargo ship, which was still quite big. Coolies were carrying bundles and boxes up the narrow wooden gangplank onto the ship. The occasional passenger hurried up carrying their own travelling trunks.

'Are we going to board the ship?' asked Lili.

'We don't want to cause a diplomatic incident by forcing our way onto a Japanese ship,' said Miss Adelia. 'Ideally, we'll intercept before Lizard's uncle boards.'

Lizard was on edge. Voices in different languages were all around him, machinery hums and clanks echoed in his ears and electric lights washed the whole area, giving everybody's faces weird shadows. Underlying everything was the ceaseless slap and splash of the sea against the dock and the hull of the ship. An image of Uncle Archie in the Tanaka's basement cage flashed through his tired, dazed mind.

'At least he won't be in chains,' said Lili, as though reading Lizard's mind. 'They won't want him drawing any attention.'

No one on the dock paid any attention to them as they stood and watched crates and boxes being taken up the gangplank.

Two coolies came past, carrying a large wooden box. 'So heavy,' one complained in Hokkien, as he staggered past. 'Should have been loaded with the crane.'

'Shut up and hold it steady,' grunted the other one.

'I am. You're the one not holding it steady,' replied the first. 'Hope we can get it up the gangplank.'

Lizard watched it go past as if in a dream. It did look heavy and wobbly.

The men had reached the gangplank before he saw the words on the box. A large label gleamed briefly as the light caught it. It said *Via Singapore*.

The coolies looked at the gangplank, complained a bit more, then hefted the box onto their shoulders, above the railings of the gangplank. They were halfway up before Lizard noticed the words stamped on the box under the *Via Singapore* label: *Tanaka's Emporium*.

He grabbed Lili's arm. 'Look!' he said, pointing at the box. 'Tanaka's Emporium!' He didn't wait for Lili's reaction before he pelted towards the gangplank.

Just as he reached it, he heard the coolies give a warning shout, and the box fell from their shoulders and tumbled over the side. It hit the water far below and broke apart.

Lizard got a glimpse of a man in the wreckage, just before he sank into the harbour. 'Uncle Archie!' Lizard yelled, and he leapt off the dock.

The cold, black water of the harbour closed over Lizard's head. He couldn't breathe and he couldn't see anything, but he could move, and his arms swept through the water, his hands searching and grabbing. Then he felt something. Hair.

He held it tight and kicked up hard. His face broke through to the surface and he gasped air deep into his lungs as he struggled to pull Uncle Archie up.

Just as he felt himself going under again he realised there was someone else in the water with him.

'All right, Lizard, I've got him now, you can let go.'

Lizard blinked and saw Mr Bee. 'Let him go so we can get you both out of the harbour, eh?'

Mr Bee prised Lizard's cold, cramping fingers out of Uncle Archie's hair. Lizard couldn't seem to let go on his own. Then Mr Bee pulled Uncle Archie away and Lizard saw that his uncle's eyes were closed and his face was white. He tried to follow, but people were hauling him up and out of the water.

Lizard sat on the concrete dock, wet and shivering and exhausted. Lili's face hovered into view and he staggered to his feet and reached out for her. She grabbed his shoulders to steady him.

'Where's Uncle Archie?' he said, searching for a glimpse of his uncle through the forest of strangers.

'He's all right, Lizard,' Lili said. 'Mr Bee has taken him away and he'll be all right.'

'Where?' said Lizard. 'Take me to him.'

'I can't. They took him away in the car, they wouldn't say where,' said Lili.

Then Lizard's legs wouldn't hold him up anymore

and he crumpled onto the dock. Somebody threw a rough towel around him, and two of the dock coolies helped him to the harbour entrance and bundled him into a rickshaw. Lili got in next to him.

'The Girls' Mission School, Sophia Road,' Lili said to the rickshaw man.

'No,' said Lizard, through chattering teeth. 'Home. The shop.'

'But, Lizard, there's a nurse at the school—' Lili started.

'*No.* Or I'll get out and walk.' He squeezed his eyes shut and lay back, pulling the towel tight around him, but he couldn't stop trembling. Was Uncle Archie all right? His face had been so pale, so unresponsive. Lizard had never seen him look like that, not even in the basement of Tanaka's Emporium. He was bereft at being separated from his uncle again, and utterly heartsick at the thought that he might have been too late to save him.

Vaguely, he was aware of arriving at the tailor shop, of being bundled up the stairs and of Lili talking to a surprised Ah Mok. Lili left the cubicle and Ah Mok dried Lizard off and helped him change his clothes.

Lili came back and pushed a warm mug of Ovaltine into his hands. She made him drink it all, and then she turned to Ah Mok and offered him twenty cents to watch Lizard overnight. She put a blanket over him. Lizard clutched it and curled up on his bunk, facing the wall, completely shattered. Why wouldn't they take him to Uncle Archie? He needed to see Uncle Archie.

Lizard had called this place home before, but tonight this cubicle didn't feel like home.

Home was curry puffs on the verandah of a stilt house in Changi.

Home was wherever Uncle Archie was.

He felt as if he would never find his way home, and disappointment crushed him like a concrete slab dropped on his chest. He was grateful for the darkness that washed over him and dragged him down into the oblivion of sleep.

CHAPTER TWENTY-TWO

Highly Useful Intelligence

Three days later, Lili stepped into the corner office on the top floor of the school. A tall man stood by the open window, looking at the view of Singapore. He turned, and Lili recognised Sir Wilbur Willoughby, Director of the Asia Division of Maximum Operations Enterprise.

'Good morning, sir,' she said.

'Lili, at last! Miss Neha and Miss Adelia have been most complimentary about your recent efforts. We are very pleased. The war office has gained extremely valuable intelligence from breaking the Japanese Navy codes. Those maps and photographs you found in the Raffles Studio show the locations of all the aerodromes in the Malay Peninsula plus new ones the Japanese army are building elsewhere and...

well, we won't be caught napping, that's for sure. You may well have saved the Empire's Jewel of the East.'

'Oh, thank you, sir,' Lili said, blushing. 'And how is Uncle—I mean the gamekeeper?'

'He is doing splendidly, and has provided highly useful intelligence,' said Sir Wilbur. 'I can't really tell you any more than that, I'm afraid.'

'But when can Lizard see him?' Lili said.

'Ah—the boy, Lizard. He's one loose end we need to tie up.' He looked Lili straight in the eye. 'I'm afraid he's a security risk. *You* are an important member of Maximum Operations Enterprise—'

'We couldn't have done it without him,' said Lili.

Sir Wilbur pressed on, as if she hadn't spoken. 'We are very grateful for his help. Nevertheless, he has knowledge that could be problematic in the wrong hands.'

'But he would never do anything wrong!' Lili said.

'My dear, I know you don't think so, but he is a thief, isn't he?' He picked up some papers from his desk and studied them. 'Mixes with the Chinatown underworld—says here he is a known associate of Wong Ah Beng, Chinatown criminal, recently deceased. Is this true?'

'But that's not all he is,' Lili protested.

'What would happen if the boy passed on information to the gunjin or the Nazis?' said Sir Wilbur. 'He is your next mission.'

'My next mission? What do you mean?' Lili said, confused.

'It's fairly simple. Your mission is to find the boy Lizard and bring him to the Changi Military Base. Don't worry, he'll be housed in plenty of comfort,' said Sir Wilbur.

'Where? For how long?' asked Lili.

'Somewhere much better than his current abode, no doubt. For as long as is necessary,' said Sir Wilbur. 'And this mission is top secret—tell no one, not even the good operatives here. These are the details.' He handed her a file. 'I know I can rely on you, Lili.'

He sat back, his eyes twinkling. 'Now off you go,' he said and he strode to the door and opened it. 'Good day, Lili,' he said, and he closed the door as soon as Lili stepped out.

Lili stood outside holding the file and thought about the conversation she had overheard between Miss Adelia and Miss Neha. Was there a detention centre at Changi? Or were they planning to lock Lizard up somewhere on the military base? Lili felt uneasy as she remembered that there was also a prison at Changi.

No, surely they wouldn't lock a boy up in the Changi Prison. Miss Adelia had told her that working for Maximum Ops wouldn't always be easy; that sometimes it would be very hard indeed.

She walked directly to Chinatown, where she knew she would find Lizard.

CHAPTER TWENTY-THREE

A Question of Freedom

'Hey, Lili!' someone called from behind her. She turned to see Lizard and Roshan walking up the road. Lizard's right cheek had a neat rectangular dressing taped to it.

'Isn't it a beautiful day?' Roshan said, as he bounced to a stop next to her.

'Why so cheerful?' Lili asked.

'That horrible pushy English girl has finally left Raffles,' Roshan replied, and he burst into a popular Tamil song, complete with vigorous arm sweeps and rhythmic jumps.

Lizard was more subdued. Even though Lili had told him that Miss Adelia said that Uncle Archie was recovering in a hospital somewhere, Lizard didn't seem to believe her, and he kept asking to see him.

'Where are you going?' Lili asked Lizard and Roshan.

'We're going to eat, and then we're going to a meeting. Want to come?' asked Roshan.

'Meeting?' said Lili, repeating the last thing that her ears had taken in. 'What meeting?'

'It is a great man! Mahatma Gandhi!' said Roshan. 'That's what my brother is telling me, anyway. At the Indian Youth Centre in Serangoon Road.'

'Who is he?' asked Lili, as if she didn't know. She looked at Lizard's face while she spoke. He looked listless, and thinner than he used to be.

'He thinks Mother India should be free!' said Roshan.

'What do you mean, *free*?' Lizard frowned.

'He says that we Indians can run our country ourselves!' Roshan dropped his voice. 'You know, free from the British!'

'What? How can that be?' Lizard said, looking puzzled. Lili was relieved that he seemed to be paying attention to something. 'They've always run things. Anyway, you were born in Singapore, not India.

You've never even been to India.'

'Well, that's true,' said Roshan, scratching his head. 'Well, all right. Freedom for Singapore then!'

'Where would we be without the British?' asked Lizard.

'Yes, where?' echoed Lili.

'Well,' said Roshan, shrugging. 'Maybe *I* could be eating at the Raffles Dining Room and an English man could be serving me!' He laughed and even Lizard raised a smile.

'Enough nonsense,' said Roshan. 'Let's go to Fatty Dim Sum's. I am free until six o'clock, then I'm back on duty: waiter wallah in the dining room, under the gaze of good King George.'

Lili looked at Lizard and Roshan. Why, she wondered, was the idea of Roshan being served by an Englishman so funny? Because the British were in charge. But why were they in charge? Why should they decide what happens? It didn't feel right. A British man had told her to bring Lizard to Changi Military Base—that's what it said in her mission brief file. What exactly was Sir Wilbur Willoughby planning for Lizard? She had to know.

'You two, go on ahead. Order me some fried rice,' said Lili. 'I'll catch up soon.'

She turned and ran all the way back to school and pelted up the stairs to the corner office. When there was no answer to her knock, she went in. Nobody was in the room. It was quiet here, except for the ticking of the wall clock and the distant hubbub of the town drifting in through the open window. She shut the door behind her.

She knew she would be expelled if she got caught, but she needed to find out what was in store for Lizard. She went to the desk. The top drawer was locked.

Was she actually going to break into the desk of Sir Wilbur Willoughby, director of the Asia Division of Maximum Operations Enterprise? She took a big breath in, pulled out her lock-picking set and went to work.

A thick file labelled 'Top Secret' was in the drawer. She opened the file and scanned the first page.

Name: Archer James Dale

Codename: The gamekeeper

She flipped through the file. Uncle Archie had been under cover for the past two years. Lili's eyes widened as she read that Uncle Archie had stolen the codebook, smuggled it into India and given it to Sebastian Whitford Jones to deliver to Commander Baxter.

Lizard had been right all along.

Lili read on. The most recent report had yesterday's date on it.

The gamekeeper is in a satisfactory condition in Changi Military Hospital.

The next page was a report on Lizard, with a photo of him attached.

Name: Lucas Zachariah Dale

Known as: Lizard

Chinese Name: 林明路

Parents: deceased

Paternal uncle: Archer James Dale (Codename 'The gamekeeper')

There were a few more lines about his school, address, and known associates, but it was the last sentence that caught Lili's eye.

Plan: Detain until further notice at Changi Military Base—withhold all information from the gamekeeper.

It was just as Lili had heard Miss Adelia and Miss Neha say. Sir Wilbur planned to lock Lizard up only because Sir Wilbur was suspicious of him, and thought he could sell secrets to the enemy.

It wasn't fair. Lizard would never do that. And Sir Wilbur was using Lili's friendship with Lizard to catch him, and he was going to hide the truth from Uncle Archie. He knew Uncle Archie wouldn't stand for it, and he needed the gamekeeper to continue his work as a spy.

Lili put the file back and locked the drawer.

Lizard and Roshan looked up as Lili came into Fatty Dim Sum's coffee shop, thoroughly out of breath.

'Hi, Lili. Where have you been? We were just about to eat your fried rice for you,' Roshan said.

Lizard pushed his noodles around on his plate.

Brylcreem and Buck Tooth came in, and sat down next to Lizard. Brylcreem draped his arm across Lizard's shoulders and dropped a sheet of paper on the table. '*Wei*, Lizard, I got the questions for the police exam. "Who is the gah-ven-ner of the Straits Settlements?"' he read. He uttered a few swear words in Hokkien. 'Who care, lah? All I want to know is where is my big wooden stick, and where do I put the bad guys?'

As Brylcreem, Buck Tooth and Roshan argued over the questions on the exam, Lili spoke to Lizard in a low voice. 'Lizard, I need you to come to Changi with me tomorrow. Bring what you need for a few days.'

'Changi?' Lizard said, surprised. 'Where in Changi? Why?'

She looked into his eyes. 'You just have to trust me,' she said.

CHAPTER TWENTY-FOUR

Curry Puffs

Lili peered in through the window of the hospital at the Changi Military Base. Only one of the four beds in the room was occupied. The building was on a hill, with a view of the sea—calm and blue today. White curtains billowed in the gentle breeze.

'*Wei*,' said Lili.

Uncle Archie dropped the book he was reading. It was a week since the Singapore Harbour incident and he looked much better than the last time she had seen him: he was now both dry and conscious. He got out of bed and came to the window.

'Hello,' he said cautiously.

'I'm Lili, Lizard's friend,' she said. 'Remember?'

'Yes, of course I remember. The lock-picker in Tanaka's. What are you doing here?' he said. 'Is

Lizard here?'

'No, but he's nearby,' she said. She had planned everything she was going to say, and she took a deep breath and began. 'Don't ask me how I know, but I need to tell you something. About Lizard.'

'Go on.' Uncle Archie leaned forward on the windowsill.

'Sir Wilbur Willoughby wants to send Lizard to the Changi detention centre and doesn't want you to know.' Lili paused, heart thumping. She was breaking Maximum Ops rules and she could be thrown out of the organisation, or worse. 'I didn't tell Lizard.'

Uncle Archie was silent, but his eyes narrowed. Uncle Archie was a top spy and he would understand all the implications.

'Where is Lizard now?' he said eventually.

'At Pak Tuah's house.'

'Excellent. Wait a moment,' he rummaged around in the drawer by his bed, found some paper and a pencil and scribbled a note. 'Can you please take this message to Pak Tuah? Tell Lizard to wait there.'

Lili nodded and took the message.

*

It was evening and the sunlight slanted gold through the smoke of the village cooking fires. The fragrance of frying fish and rice cooking in coconut milk was in the air.

Lili sat on Pak Tuah's verandah.

Lizard, unable to sit still, was climbing the nearest palm tree, his satchel slung around to his back. He was halfway up the trunk when Uncle Archie came up from the beach, carrying a holdall. Lizard slid down off the tree and sprinted towards him.

'Uncle Archie!' he cried, flinging his arms around him.

Uncle Archie laughed and hugged him tightly. 'It's so good to see you, Lizard. So very, very good.'

Uncle Archie let go of Lizard and stood back to look at him. 'You're looking a bit thin,' he said. 'You need to eat more.'

'So do you, Uncle Archie.' Lizard was unable to stop smiling. He gripped his uncle's hand and his heart brimmed with joy.

Pak Tuah came out of the house and Uncle Archie

went to him.

'Mr Archie, *selamat kembali*,' Pak Tuah said. Welcome back.

'Thank you, Pak Tuah, old friend, and thank you for all your help,' said Uncle Archie.

'I have arranged everything as you requested,' Pak Tuah said. 'My cousin will be here soon.' He smiled at Lizard. 'This young man has been waiting a long time to see you.' He lit the lamp on the verandah and went back into the house.

'I have something for you,' Uncle Archie said, opening his holdall. He took out a paper-wrapped parcel.

'What's that?' said Lizard

'Curry puffs,' said Uncle Archie, breaking into the parcel. 'Not from Chinatown, though. Turns out there's a local chap who does curry puffs over in the Chinese village. Sorry, they're so late.'

Lizard's mouth dropped open.

'You do still like curry puffs, don't you?' said Uncle Archie, as the savoury aroma wafted out.

Lizard stared at his uncle. There was so much he

wanted to say, but he just nodded. He took a curry puff and bit into it.

'Any good?' asked Uncle Archie.

'It's perfect,' said Lizard with his mouth full. 'Absolutely perfect.'

'Excellent,' said Uncle Archie, with a grin.

'I have something for you, too.' Lizard opened his satchel and took out the dark blue trilby. He had carefully stuffed a shirt in it so that the hat wouldn't get squashed out of shape.

'Your favourite hat,' said Lizard. 'I kept it for you.'

Uncle Archie cleared his throat as he took the hat from Lizard and put it on his head. 'It still fits,' he said. 'Thank you, Lizard.'

Lili moved over to make room on the verandah and Uncle Archie and Lizard sat down.

Uncle Archie turned to Lizard. 'I've organised for you to stay at a place out of Singapore. We need to get you away from here, for your safety.'

'I'm leaving Singapore?' said Lizard, looking at his uncle. 'Are you coming too?'

'I'll go with you tonight to see you settled in, then I have to come back and sort out some business, but only for a day or two,' Uncle Archie said.

'But why?' said Lizard. 'Why can't you stay with me? I don't understand,' said Lizard, frowning.

'I'll tell you on the way,' said Uncle Archie. 'Go and say goodbye to Pak Tuah.'

Uncle Archie watched Lizard go inside.

Lili looked at Uncle Archie's serious face, and didn't want to hear what he was going to tell her.

'Lili, thank you. I'm very much in your debt,' he said.

'Where are you taking him?' asked Lili, though she knew what the answer would be.

'It's best if I don't tell you, don't you think?' he said gently. 'It won't be forever, Lili. Maybe a few months. Sir Wilbur isn't going to waste valuable resources looking too hard for him—and soon he'll have far more important things to worry about.'

Lili nodded and looked out over the track that led to the sea. The sun had set now, and a crescent moon was rising.

Uncle Archie said, 'We'll just tell him Lizard's disappeared and we don't know where he is.'

Lili knew that Lizard would be gone for at least a few months, but uncertain times were coming and war was looming—she didn't know when she would see him again.

'Sir Wilbur's not going to be happy,' said Uncle Archie, 'when you tell him you can't find Lizard.'

'I know,' Lili said. 'Do you think I'll get expelled?'

'I doubt it. You're trained and valuable. And Sir Wilbur won't want any fuss. I'll tell him Lizard's disappeared and I don't know where he is,' said Uncle Archie. 'People go missing all the time.'

Lili nodded. Uncle Archie's words were reassuring, so she didn't know why she felt so bereft.

Lizard came out onto the verandah.

'Are you ready to go?' Uncle Archie said to him.

Lizard picked up his satchel. 'Yes. Let's go.'

'Don't you have something to say?' Uncle Archie nudged Lizard, and went down the steps, leaving

Lizard and Lili on the verandah.

'Bye, Lili,' said Lizard. It struck him that he didn't know when he was going to see her next, or Chinatown, or his school, or Fatty Dim Sum or Ah Mok or Brylcreem or anyone he knew. He was going somewhere unknown with Uncle Archie, and trusting only Uncle Archie—and that was all right with him.

'If you need anything, let me know,' said Lili.

Lizard looked at Lili's face, and remembered how she had found him his cubicle home, and a school and helped him find Uncle Archie. 'Thank you for everything. I'll never be able to repay you,' he said.

'Well, I don't know,' Lili said, her eyes glistening in the lamplight. 'My English is much better now, so I think we are even already. Go on, he's waiting for you.'

Lizard thought about hugging her, but that was ridiculous. Shaking her hand? No, even more ridiculous. He dithered back and forth a bit more before raising a hand and waving.

'Bye,' he said, and he turned and ran down the

steps to Uncle Archie.

'Want another curry puff?' Uncle Archie said, reaching into the paper parcel.

'Sure,' said Lizard. As he bit into the fragrant, still-warm curry puff, he was happy in a way he hadn't been for a very long time.

Uncle Archie took the trilby off his head and dropped it onto Lizard's. 'I think it looks better on you,' he said.

Lizard tilted it at a jaunty angle. 'You're probably right.'

Uncle Archie laughed and cuffed his head.

The palm trees rustled in the sea breeze as they headed across the beach. The moon cast a pale glow, illuminating a motorboat that was puttering in to shore.

'We're going in a boat?' Lizard asked.

'Yes,' Uncle Archie said, through a mouthful of pastry flakes.

Lizard looked back and saw Lili standing in the lamplight on the verandah, watching him go. Fireflies were moving sparks in the darkness and the stars glimmered overhead. All the lights blurred together as he waved one last time, and turned to face the future with Uncle Archie by his side.

Glossary

aiyah (Cantonese*) — exclamation to show dismay or surprise

aiyoh (Mandarin) — exclamation to show mild annoyance

alamak (Malay) — expression of surprise or shock

amah (Portuguese derivation) — Cantonese domestic helper

cheen (Cantonese) — money

dai goh (Cantonese) — big brother

deem ah (Cantonese) — how are you?

genmaicha (Japanese) — green tea combined with roasted rice

gunjin (Japanese) — a person in the military

kagi (Japanese) — key

konbanwa (Japanese) — good evening

kurippu (Japanese) clip

kway teow (Hokkien) — fried thick, flat rice-noodle dish

lah (Cantonese) — placed at the end of a phrase for emphasis *matte kudasai* (Japanese) — wait, please

nan desu ka? (Japanese) — what is it?

poh piah (Teochew) — thin pancake rolled and stuffed with a savoury filling

san (Japanese) — honorific used after a name, which can mean Mr, Mrs, Miss or Ms

selamat kembali (Malay) — welcome back

tanto (Japanese) — a straight-bladed dagger

uguisu (Japanese) — a bush warbler often kept as a cage bird for its song

wallah (Hindi) — a person concerned with a specific business

yuuki ne? (Japanese) — brave, eh?

*Colloquial Cantonese has been rendered into English phonetically.

Author's Note

The events of *Lizard's Tale* occur about thirteen months before the real-life bombing of Singapore by the Imperial Japanese Navy Air Force, on 8 December 1941. The Imperial Japanese Army then occupied Singapore until September 1945, when WWII officially ended.

In pre-war Singapore, spies and agents collected information for Japan in preparation for the impending conflict. There was a photography studio at Raffles Hotel run for many years before the war by a Mr Nakajima. He was employed by the *Straits Times* newspaper and was the official photographer for the British naval base. People were surprised to see him during the war as a lieutenant colonel in the Imperial Japanese Army, and it was claimed that he was a Japanese intelligence officer. This mysterious figure is the basis for the fictional Mr Nakajima in this story.

Mr Shinozaki, the man who tried to get Lizard

to leave Tanaka's Emporium, is based on the real-life Shinozaki Mamoru, who was put in Changi Prison by the British in 1940 for espionage and only released when the Japanese took control of Singapore. After his release he saved many local people during the war. According to his autobiography, the army gave him the job of protecting Germans (as Germany was allied to Japan) and 'good citizens' from bad treatment by the Japanese authorities. Shinozaki decided to give out passes to anyone who asked him, to protect them from beatings or imprisonment, risking his own safety.

Several other fictional characters in *Lizard's Tale* are based on real historical figures. Mr Arathoon managed Raffles Hotel for many years, even during the Japanese occupation. Sir Arthur Percival was a senior British Army officer who played an important part in the war in Malaya, although he wasn't in Singapore at the time *Lizard's Tale* is set. Sir William Dobbie was General Officer Commanding Malaya until 1939. King George VI and Emperor Hirohito were the reigning monarchs of their empires in 1940.

All the events in which these characters appear in *Lizard's Tale* are fictitious.

Acknowledgments

There are many people I would like to thank.

My father Keng Mow, who grew up in a shop house in Tanjong Pagar, which exists only in memories and photographs and now also in *Lizard's Tale*. The family home and tailor shop were downstairs, but I never got to see what the floor above was like in real life.

My mother Siu Chee, who gave us comics and started us on a lifelong love of books.

My sister Weng Chyn and my brother Weng Key, for being terrific and reliable (and still just a bit annoying sometimes—love you, guys).

My Singapore relatives for being welcoming and endearingly honest in the Cantonese way.

I'm grateful to those who gave me feedback: Janice Marriott, Cath Mayo, Robin Harding, Ana Sharpe, Lisa Grace and Lindsey Dawson, also to Tony Hill, Melinda Hii, Megan Cartwright and Jamie Cartwright.

Thanks to Leanne Hall for saying nice things about my book, and writing lovely books for young people.

Thanks to Mandy Brett, for choosing my manuscript, Imogen Stubbs for the beautiful cover design and Sarah Allen for the gorgeous illustration, and to Jamila Khodja, Anne Beilby, Stefanie Italia, Khadija Caffoor, Emily Booth, Shalini Kunahlan, Patti Patcha and all at Text. I'm especially grateful to Jane Pearson, whose editing was terrifying and wonderful.

Thanks to my dear friends Lynda, Bhavana and Fiona (I miss you).

Love always to Amelia, Olivia and Samantha for lighting up my life in brilliant colours.

For Marty, your steadfast and loving support means the world to me.

Thanks to God, who makes everything possible.